Soul
RESURRECTION

Soul RESURRECTION

SOUL WEAVER DUOLOGY BOOK ONE

CHANTELLE LAMBERT

Identifiers:
ISBN-13: 978-0-6488867-4-7 (paperback 5x8in)
ISBN-13: 978-0-6488867-8-5 (paperback 5.5x8.5in)
ISBN-13: 978-0-6488867-9-2 (hardback)
ISBN-13: 978-0-6488867-3-0 (e-book)

Available in paperback, hardback, and e-book.

Book Cover Design by
Creya-tive Book Cover Design
www.creya-tive.com

To my loving husband for being with me through my depression and anxiety.

You are my light in the darkness.

NORTH TOWER POINT

MYRDREYA

THE RIDGE PASS

MOUNT SEASIDE

MORVIK

ELVANOR FOREST

DARK CASTLE

NIRDRA

SOUTH TOWER POINT

ZALINDOR

Prologue

TRIXIE

WITH ONE FOOT AFTER THE other, I zigzagged through the dense trees. Intertwined roots and thick undergrowth tangled around my ankles. I twisted my feet to break free. A large decaying tree, long been dead and forgotten, leaned on a moss-covered boulder. I dropped to the muddy vegetation and rolled under the stone. Scrambling, I pushed myself off the ground and hauled my body over more fallen trees.

Cloaked by darkness, a thin branch hung low, crossing

my path. It struck me square in the face. A groan escaped my lips as I jolted backward. Cupping my hand over my mouth, I stared wide eyed behind me. *Shit. Had they heard?* Warm blood dripped down my cold cheek. I was certain the cut was deep. I didn't have a spare second to check.

The moon shafts made it through the impenetrable canopy—the only light visible. I couldn't see my feet as they crunched dead leaves—let alone see the direction I stepped. My muscles quivered. *What had I been thinking?* That was the problem; I mustn't have been thinking at all when I jumped through.

Thump. Thump. Pounding in my ears.

I pressed my back into a tree trunk. Staring wildly around, I looked for my next course of action.

Thump. Thump. Drumming in my chest.

Leaning against the trunk with my forearm, I peered around it.

"You can't hide!" A man thundered from their ranks; I could hear the smirk in his voice.

Muscles trembling, I pushed away from my short-lived hiding place. Shouted words continued to reach my ears. I didn't pay any attention to what they said. They were closing in—too close for comfort. I forced my legs to speed up.

"Give up already," another man's voice sounded, closer this time.

The moist air made it difficult to breathe. The trees'

proximity made it tricky to determine which way to go. *How was I going to escape them?* My foot snagged under a tree root, and I almost toppled over. I reached out for support, grabbing the nearest tree to steady myself. Gasping for air, I clutched my chest. I compelled myself to keep moving despite my growing anxiety, bloody face and my now throbbing foot.

Lacking oxygen, I ran for my life.

If they caught me, I was as good as dead.

A shiver coursed down my spine. One of them was getting close on my heels. I refused to look back, forcing myself to focus on forward movement. Winding my way through the forest, I leapt over small boulders and broken branches. Twigs and more dead leaves crushed under my feet—and moments later, under the feet of my closest pursuer.

Thump. Thump.

My heart hammered as I ducked under another low-hanging branch. Catching my foot on one more tree root, I stumbled. The ground came closer to my face as I fell to the earth, collapsing onto my hands and knees. I whimpered as my palm came into contact with a sharp rock, slicing it open—instantly reminded of the wound on my face. They both stung.

The hunter was upon me, grabbing my shoulders and rolling me over. He pinned me to the forest floor. Damp dirt mushed into my hair, and a sharp stick dug into my back. I wriggled under his weight as he straddled me, holding my wrists down. My unsteady breath escaped my lips as I thrashed beneath him.

"Let...me..."

"Trix?" The sound of his voice startled me.

Hearing my nickname, I stopped struggling against him and stared up at his face. My breath caught in my throat as my mouth fell open. I focused on the familiar face, my eyes growing wide. His dark skin, cheekbones, jawline, and ice-blue eyes were how I remembered them. I couldn't believe who was staring back down at me.

FOUR MONTHS EARLIER

One

*H*IS BODY PRESSED AGAINST MY back; muscles contracted as he leaned over and kissed my shoulder. His mouth slid gently across my skin, resting at my neck—the soft touch of his lips sent trembles down my spine.

A soft moan escaped my throat as I tilted my head away so he could continue kissing my neck. Reaching my arms up, I tangled my petite hands in his short wavy hair, which was as dark as night. My body became heavy as I leaned into him, allowing him to take over me. I lost my mind in his touch. His hands were sliding over my body — my arms, my stomach, my thighs. I tingled.

Then the warmth and pressure of his body against mine were gone. I lost balance, almost tumbling over. I regained my footing and turned around to look at him — but he wasn't there.

I glanced around the room and felt my breathing become laboured and my heart thumping inside my rib cage. I stood alone.

"Levi?" I called out.

My bedroom door was half-open — *had we left it open like that?* I couldn't remember. I hurried across the room. My heart still pounded from the intimate moment we had been having; a new tightness growing inside.

A car engine kicked over on the street; my face drained of colour. As I darted down the hallway, I saw the front door was ajar. I hurried forward, pushing it wide-open. Looking out over the front lawn, I saw his black sedan driving away down the street. I stared in disbelief as his car turned the corner and disappeared from view.

I stood there for a moment, stunned. A cool breeze touched my skin and made me shiver. Turning back to my house, I slowly strolled back in, closing the door behind me.

Why had he left so suddenly? My brows furrowed. Standing in my living room, I could hear my heart throbbing in my ears. It felt like it would explode right out of my body.

I rushed back to my bedroom, scooping up my phone

from the bedside table. Dialling his phone number, I paced around the room.

Beep, beep, beep.

I tried calling him several times. No answer. I threw my phone onto my bed. The silence was deafening.

My bedroom walls caved in; the architecture bending and warping at odd angles. I stood in the room alone as it shrank. The weight of the four walls crushed down on me as my world fell apart—again.

I collapsed onto the end of my queen-sized bed; the emptiness swallowing me. My chest tightened further. I couldn't get the air into my lungs. The room was whirling around me—*or was it my head spinning?* I wasn't sure. I gripped the blankets with my fingers as dizziness took over. Squeezing my eyes shut, I took a deep breath and reopened them. The walls weren't crushing anymore. I gazed around my bedroom; everything was back in place.

I always had a wild imagination. My mind would make up events that never even happened. A few years after my parents had disappeared, I accepted my diagnosis of depression and anxiety. Not lightly, though; it wasn't easy to be told that I had a metal illness. Levi had healed most of my wounds, but the depression still crept up on me when I least expected it.

Staring out the window, I could see leaves in the trees rustling in the winter wind. I considered the details of our intimate moment. *Had I done something wrong?* A tear slipped from the corner of my eye; my vision blurred.

Tracing my fingertips over the skin on my neck that his lips had touched, memories flashed across my eyes — beautiful memories, painful memories. I didn't understand why he had left suddenly, without so much as a whisper.

⋙ ◉ ⋘

THE NEXT FEW days passed silently as my anxiety grew. I still hadn't heard from Levi. I continued calling him and messaging him, but there was never an answer. It was like he had vanished from earth.

Heart aching with grief, I was plummeting into misery. *Would I ever see his pale blue eyes on me again?* Trembling from head to toe, I was frightened of being alone again. The thought of my four walls closing in on me to the point of no return terrified me.

On the fourth day of his absence, when I called him, a message informed me that his phone number had been disconnected. My breath caught in my throat; airways constricted and burned. I sunk to my knees, clutching at my neck. Dizziness made my temples pound.

I couldn't comprehend why he had abandoned me. I pressed my palm against my chest, trying to suppress my sorrow. My heart was bleeding, crushed by the man I thought had been the love of my life. Since he had disappeared, I had not smiled; I couldn't.

He had vanished; it was like he never existed. *Was I*

crazy? Had he ever existed? Had I made it all up? It had felt so real. My stomach lurched; I felt queasy. My body ached for his touch. I began seeing stars before my body collapsed and everything turned black.

A FEW LONELY months passed. I was broken. My life was falling apart. I didn't know how to smile anymore. My eyes had dried up, too; no more tears to cry.

I spent most days curled up under the blankets, cuddling a pillow for comfort. I only forced myself out of bed when I had to—to get groceries, eat, go to the bathroom, or to work. Being an editor, I worked from home. Though I used to love editing books, since Levi had left, I was moving through life as if I was a robot. I had emotionally and mentally chained myself inside.

Old feelings of despair and self-hatred were creeping back in. I was, once again, beginning to question whether life was worth living. Returning to those dark, lonely, lost days was the last thing I wanted to do.

Falling deeper into depression, and already struggling with the loss of my parents, Levi leaving tipped me over the edge. My parents' abandonment had ripped out my heart and soul. Over the years, I lived a relatively normal life sprinkled with occasional breakdowns. Levi had healed my heart from the loss of my parents, but my soul had remained torn apart.

But now I had lost Levi as well, and the haemorrhage in my heart had returned. My chest was feeling like it might explode with emotion.

Then everything was numb.

Two

"WHAT A BORING LIFE," I whispered to myself as I ran my fingers through my short brown hair.

I had been crouched on this tree branch for a while. It definitely wasn't the most comfortable place or position, but there was nowhere else to hide. The large oak I was perched in was leafy enough to keep me out of her sight.

The night air seeped through my black clothes and a shiver rolled down my spine; I clearly hadn't dressed appropriately tonight. Autumn had vanished and winter was creeping in. I longed for my bed, where it was warm. *How long had I been sitting here?* Definitely hours. If it had snowed in this little town, I would have been frozen to the bone. I rubbed my hands together, wishing I had brought gloves with me.

Watching Trixie was currently the purpose of my existence — and she was *boring,* with a capital B. Every day she just stared at nothingness or she would sit at the dining table hunched over her laptop for hours on end.

Tonight, she had been sitting in the same chair for the last hour, staring at nothing. *What on earth was she doing?* It was like she was in a trance or extremely deep in thought. I wasn't sure if she had blinked in the past minute.

Tapping my foot on the tree trunk with impatience, I groaned. *Why had I received the dullest mission in existence?* Others were off tracking the Soul Hunters, but I was stuck watching a human who was boring me to tears.

At least she was half decent to look at — pity about the untidy clothes and messy hair, though. And her house...it was like children lived in it, not an adult. Over the past few months of watching her, I hadn't seen her clean — not once. Well, maybe wash a cup or plate, but that was all.

Oh, she's finally moving! Gripping the trunk with one hand, I leaned on a thick branch with the other. I watched as she stood from her living room chair and made her way to...the bathroom. Clearing my throat, I looked away and leaned back against the tree trunk. Well, that was unexciting.

Every minute of the day that I watched her, she stared off into the distance; it was like she was hollow or not there at all. No one visited her, at least not while I was protecting her house. She was always sitting alone, doing absolutely nothing. There were rare times I saw her perched over a laptop for hours on end, but I could never see what she was doing.

There had been no sign of danger this whole time of guarding her house. This was pointless. She had shown no indication of being unique, so I didn't understand why I had to waste my time guarding her.

Sighing, I jumped down from the large oak tree and pressed my body against the trunk. Peering around it, I quickly checked she wasn't in sight before I hurried away.

After strolling a few streets away, I came to face the forest I had originally entered this little town from. I knew the forest well now, having travelled through it every day for the past few months.

Moon-shafts peered through the thick canopy, lighting up patches of the forest. I avoided walking through the light, keeping to the shadows. A small rodent scurried away as I approached, and an owl hooted far in the distance. I stopped and squinted into the trees ahead. Pushing forward with my senses, there was a body standing behind a trunk ahead.

"Hi, Jake." I said, smirking.

He sighed and stepped around the tree. "You're too good."

"Exactly why I should be out there scouting, not here watching a worthless human." I grumbled as I reached my best friend's side.

Jake and I had known each other since I landed in Myrdreya when I was sixteen; eight years ago.

"She might not be as worthless as you think." He said as we strolled further into the forest.

"Pfft," I scoffed. "You haven't been up in that cold tree watching her for months on end."

"No, but I've been with Demetri." He said.

I raised an eyebrow.

"He thinks she's their daughter."

"No way." I snorted, looking at Jake.

Jake's expression was hard.

"You believe it?" I said.

"What else is there to believe?" He replied. "She could be dangerous."

"Dangerous?" I laughed. "She hasn't even got an inkling of magic."

"No magic?"

"Doubtful." I said.

"If they've found her, they will teach her and get her on their side," Jake said.

I shook my head. "She's definitely not on their side."

"How do you know?"

"She sits around her house all day, never cleans, barely ever leaves the house." I said. "She's done nothing at all to show she's anything but human."

"Hmm." Jake frowned. "Well, Demetri is adamant that she's the daughter."

I jumped over a small boulder. "I guess it would explain why I was ordered to guard her."

"Yeah, except we haven't found anything new on their whereabouts."

"Nothing at all?" I asked.

"Nothing." Jake said as we entered a small clearing in the trees.

He scanned the trees with his eyes, and I followed suit.

"Clear." He said.

I nodded, "clear."

Jake lifted his hand in front of his body and, after a moment, lime-green weaved from his fingers to form a portal. He gestured toward it, and I stepped forward.

"See you on the other side." I grinned, clapping him on the shoulder.

Jake rolled his eyes, and I stepped through.

Three

*E*ARLY ON A SATURDAY MORNING, my eyes stared at the ceiling. Winter had snuck up on me; it felt like only a week ago had been summer. I couldn't remember Autumn happening. *Had I slept through it?* Probably. Snuggled under my blankets, I debated with myself whether I could be bothered to get out of bed or not.

Thump, thump, thump.

I froze—my muscles tensed, and my jaw locked as I listened. Not a moment later, there was another knock, louder the second time. The front door. I bolted upright, tossing the bedding off my body. I was already clothed in a singlet and leggings from the day before — or the week before. Or was it from the month before? I frowned as I struggled to remember what day it was. Regardless, I hurried down the hallway.

Pulse quickening, I adjusted my clothing. I clasped the doorknob just as a third knock sounded. Whomever it was, sounded impatient. Turning the knob, I wrenched the door open.

"Trixie!" my friend exclaimed from the doorstep, flustered. Eyes wide, she fidgeted with her fingers and bit her lip.

"Kiarra." I stared at the rusty red-haired girl in front of me — my best friend.

A chilly breeze blew in and I wrapped my arms around myself. I groaned inwardly; my warm bed was calling to me.

"Are you okay?" she questioned, her eyebrows squeezed together.

"Yes, I-I thought you were…never mind…" I trailed off; I couldn't say his name.

I watched her face as she trailed my body up and down, her blue eyes observing. Shifting uncomfortably in the doorway, I stared back at her worried expression. My bones ached with longing. I should have known it wouldn't be him. My shoulders slumped with disappointment. I hoped she didn't notice.

Kiarra had been my lifelong friend since we met in the street at five years old. She had lived across the road from me, and we spent every day together after school and on weekends. When my parents disappeared and I had been sent to an orphanage, we lost contact. We reconnected again the day she walked into the cafe where I worked as a young teenager.

Kiarra had such a dominant nature that other children stayed away from her; little did they know, she had a heart of gold. She always meant well, and she was always looking out for me.

"You look like you haven't showered in a week," she stated, indicating my greasy, bird nest hair.

I put a hand on my unnaturally white blonde hair; my fingers caught in the matted mess. It must have looked gross and neglected to Kiarra. Absentmindedly, I turned and wandered into the lounge room, picking up a jacket I had left sitting over the back of the chair. Kiarra followed, closing the front door behind her. She stared at me, her fingers pulled each other again. I averted my eyes, avoiding her piercing glare, as I slipped into the jacket. An empty feeling sat in the pit of my stomach, and I bit my lip nervously.

"You actually haven't showered in a week, have you?" she asked after a minute. "Or longer…"

Her eyes watched me as I avoided answering her. I gazed around the room. It was then I noticed the state of disarray my house was in. Oh, god. Dirty plates and bowls were sitting on the coffee table; a half-drunk glass of soft drink sat on the side table next to the armchair. Blu-ray movies and books scattered on the floor and lounge chair, and there were empty chip and chocolate wrappers amongst them.

My house was a small one-bedroom townhouse; it was roomy enough for one person—me. Furnishings comprised the bare essentials that I needed to live. I was lucky to be living on the cheap side of town, so the rent was low enough for me to afford it.

In the lounge room, there was a navy blue lounge chair with a matching armchair; both of which I had picked up in a garage sale. A side table provided a place for a drink and a TV remote. The television rested on a small stand, with the Blu-ray player underneath it. A bookshelf sat against the wall, full of my favourite books; among them was *The Medoran Chronicles by Lynette Noni*, *The Twilight Saga by Stephenie Meyer*, and *The Mortal Instruments by Cassandra Clare*. I loved reading—well, I used to. I hadn't read in months.

"Trixie…Trixie!" Kiarra hollered.

I jumped in surprise. She must have been trying to get my attention while I was staring at the mess. I looked at her blankly. I wasn't really seeing her, though. My mind was far away. Robotic—what my life had become since Levi had left. I cringed at the thought of him. A month after he had disappeared, I asked Kiarra if she had ever seen him. She told me she had, proving to me he had been real. But I still wondered if I had made it all up. I blinked rapidly, pushing his face to the back of my mind.

Kiarra had a notably concerned expression on her tanned face. Her hair was tied back in a puffy ponytail, which was an unusual look for her.

"You don't usually wear your hair up." I frowned at her.

"Trixie, I am worried about you," she stated bluntly, ignoring my comment.

"I'm fine."

"No, you're not. You are pretending you're fine, but I know you aren't. I mean...look at your house." She opened her arms wide, indicating my lounge room.

I shifted uncomfortably. "I just haven't had time to clean this week."

"This week?" She raised her perfectly plucked eyebrows. "You haven't cleaned in at least a month."

She walked over to the bookshelf and slid a finger along the top of it. She held up her finger to me. A thick layer of dust.

"Or months." She emphasised the s.

I swallowed and glanced around the room again. Okay, maybe she was right.

My muscles were weak as I stood awkwardly in front of my best friend. Running my hands through my greasy, knotted hair, I sighed. I bundled my hair up as if I was going to tie it up.

Kiarra gasped.

"What is *that*?" she stared wide-eyed at me.

I dropped my hands, letting my hair fall back around my shoulders. I looked behind me to see what she was staring at. When I turned back, she was standing exceedingly close to me. I froze. She grabbed my chin, forcing me to look left, and lifted my hair on the right side of my head. Exposing my neck, she ran a finger over my skin, sending chills down my spine.

"What are you doing?" I asked as I tried turning back to her, but she held my chin in place.

She stared at my neck in bewilderment.

"How long have you had that for?" she questioned, finally releasing me.

She took a step backwards, waiting for my answer.

I stared at her, more confused than she looked.

"Had what?"

"That mark on your neck. It's like a tattoo...but not."

"Mark?" I questioned.

Placing my hand on my neck, I felt the skin, but it felt normal.

"Go have a shower," Kiarra demanded, "and then have a look in the mirror."

I grumbled, but didn't argue. Leaving Kiarra in the lounge room, I made my way to the shower.

The hot water running over my pale skin was relaxing. I listened to the water pour over me for a long moment. The rivulets of warm water followed the curves and crevices of my body. It felt like I hadn't showered in a year. I'd forgotten how much I actually enjoyed a nice cleansing shower. Wriggling my toes in the water, I gazed down as a few weeks' worth of dirt washed off.

I closed my eyes, letting the hot water run over my face. Levi's face swam behind my lids, like it did every time I closed them. I dug my nails into my scalp to stop the memories of him. *Why does it have to be so agonising? If he's not coming back, why can't his memories vanish?* I shook my head, trying to make the memories dissipate.

After my shower, I pulled on a thin pair of long, black cotton pants and a dark blue tank-top. I ran the comb through my clean, damp hair until it was smoothly draping down my back.

Looking at the girl in the mirror, I watched as her ocean blue eyes stared back at me. She was a stranger to me—an imposter—but she was me, and I was unrecognisable.

I hesitated before pushing my hair aside. My eyes broadened at seeing the milky-white, translucent mark on my neck. Kiarra hadn't been joking. My chest tightened, and my breathing sped up. I had never noticed it before. *How long had it been there?* Swirls and lines formed the interesting design that I hadn't seen before. It looked like a fancy W with a sideways swirl that formed an S. I ran my fingers over it; it was smooth as if there was nothing there.

Feeling uneasy, I shook my head and reluctantly made my way back down the hall to Kiarra.

"Definitely needed that shower," I called out to her, but there was no response.

I entered the lounge room and froze in place. My whole body trembled, my breathing caught in my throat. My eyes darted from Kiarra to the man behind her – a tall, masculine man with the body of a wrestler. He was standing in the middle of the room with one hand holding Kiarra around her shoulders and the other around her neck.

I stared in terror, my body visibly and violently shaking. The sound of my heartbeat thrashing in my ears. The man, barely 10 years older than me, stared back with pure evil in his eyes. He had a strange, dark sense to him; his hair was jet black, and his eyes were mostly black too. My eyes scanned over him, checking for visible weapons, but saw none.

Kiarra had tears running down her cheeks. Her eyes were filled with terror, and she was screaming silently for help. She didn't struggle. She was completely submissive in his grasp. *Had he beaten her into submission? Did he have more than a physical hold over her?* I have never seen her like this – the pure fear in her eyes – it was haunting.

His words snapped me out of my train of thought, back to the moment at hand.

"I've been looking for you." The man's voice was a gravelly, heavy baritone.

My muscles were tense; my blood had turned to ice. I stared at the horror in Kiarra's eyes, yet I couldn't move.

My own eyes glazed over; I didn't know what to do.

"You've been difficult to track down. But, thanks to your little friend mumbling your name in the cafe this morning... I found you." He said.

"Who are you? What do you want?" I croaked.

The side of the man's mouth contorted upward into a grin — a horrible, menacing grin.

"Oh, you won't need to know, as you will be dead before anyone comes to your rescue." His voice was taunting.

"Please, don't hurt her. Let her go." I pleaded. "She won't tell anyone."

His smirk widened. "The last little bitch I let escape my grip yelled down the street. I won't make that mistake again."

"Please." I said again, tears welling up in my eyes.

He shifted slightly, cocking his head to the side, as if to get a better look at me. With one swift movement, he jerked his hands, and a dreaded snapping noise followed.

"KIARRA! Nooooo!" I screamed as I saw the life torn from my best friend's body. Her limp form fell to the floor; her neck at an odd angle.

The man didn't even look at Kiarra as she fell; he kept his eyes on me. A bitter taste formed in my mouth as the tears spilled down my cheeks. *Not my best friend, too.* My jaw was trembling with rage and sadness; I felt an unfamiliar resolve wash over me like the warm water of my hot shower.

He stepped toward me. I snapped my gaze in his direction and put my hand up in defiance—but something more happened. I watched my fingers in surprise as they lit up with some kind of swirly electricity. My lips parted as I gasped in shock. The man jolted backward. The electric current from my fingertips quickly formed into a ball. It hurled toward the man without me even throwing it.

I watched in slow motion as the electric ball hit him in the shoulder. His mouth wrenched open in pain. Toppling over, he fell to the ground ever so slowly. *Had time just slowed down?*

As he hit the ground, it was as if the world returned to normal speed again.

My head spun; I clutched it as if I needed to hold it together. *What on Earth had just happened?* Fatigue washed through my body; strength drained from me instantly. I glanced from the man to my lifeless best friend. The man's arm moved; he was coming around. I looked at Kiarra one last time, before I escaped out the front door into the street. The street was quiet—I guessed everyone must have been at work—not one neighbour in sight.

It was broad daylight, and I was barefoot, having not even taken time to throw on footwear. It wasn't safe to stay; I had to get away from this murdering stranger.

I raced down the street as fast as my feet would carry me. The man yelled out something from behind; his deep, rasping voice reaching deep into my being and chilling me inside and out. I couldn't decipher what he said. I'm sure it was English. But my fear, and the sound of my heart hammering in my chest and my feet pounding the tarmac, drowned out whatever abuse or command he had thrown my way. Refusing to look back, I turned left up another street and could hear his boots closing the distance between us. *How was he so fast?*

Spotting an alleyway, I made a beeline for it, turning right and dashing down the narrow passage. My breathing laboured, and loose gravel in the alley was making running very painful. The stones pointed into the soles of my feet, causing me to wince and groan. I was losing momentum fast.

The winter's air was freezing on my skin. Wishing I had put a sweater on, I glanced behind me and saw him only metres away. He stopped in his tracks, standing with his feet wide apart.

I slowed my footsteps as I followed his gaze; he was staring ahead of me. Another man — dressed all in black. I planted my feet down and scanned from my purser to the dark newcomer now in front of me. I could hear my heart pounding in my ears. *Could this get any worse?* Sandwiched between them, trapped. Nowhere to go. My feet hurt; I wondered if they were bleeding.

"Duck," the newcomer bellowed in a strong, commanding tone.

Not needing to be told twice, I dropped to the ground as a glowing, purple fireball flew over my head — at least that was what I thought I saw. I felt the heat radiate across me as the fireball erupted against my pursuer's chest. He crumbled and sagged, collapsing to the ground. Still crouched on the ground, emotions overcame me as tears welled up in my eyes, again spilling down my flushed cheeks.

Strong, gentle hands grabbed me, heaving me to my feet. A gasp escaped my lips. Through my tears, I stared at the man who had launched the fireball. I looked from his brown almond-shaped eyes to the strands of his dark brown hair that had fallen out of place on his forehead. His skin was so darkly tanned, as if he had spent his life in the sun. I wiped my eyes with the back of my hand.

"Let's go," he stated abruptly, turning briskly away.

"But—"

"—No time to explain. He will wake up in a few minutes, and we have to get you out of here."

Not knowing what else to do, I paused to assess the situation. The unconscious man had just murdered my friend, and the man in front of me had saved my life. I wrestled with the idea of going back to my home, eager to find out if Kiarra really had left me. I couldn't bear the thought of life without her, too. If it hadn't been for this man, I probably would have been murdered along with Kiarra. But I did not know who he was.

"My name is Kieran." His expression softened as I glanced up at him.

Kieran held out his hand toward me. I looked at it, not

sure whether to shake it or take it. I couldn't think straight. I placed a hand on my head as I glanced from the unconscious murderer to the stunning man in front of me. A chilly breeze flowed down the alleyway, triggering my body to shiver, and my skin to burst with goosebumps.

He took a step forward and reached his hand to mine. Grasping my hand, I allowed him to lead me down the alleyway. Once we were out in the street, he started running, pulling me along beside him.

"Hurry," he stated, "we don't want him to follow."

"Who was that man and why was he –" I choked on my words, the cool air drying my throat out; the running contributed to the dryness too.

"I'm sorry about your friend." He genuinely sounded sad for me, his brisk tone all but gone.

My eyebrows pulled together as the skin on my forehead creased. I didn't tell him about Kiarra. *Where had he come from? How did he know I had been in danger?* My head whirled; so many unanswered questions – questions I wanted answers to.

"How –?" I began.

"I will explain everything when we are in a safe place," he promised.

We hurried through the streets, toward a forest. I paused at the edge of the thick line of trees, pulling my hand out of his grip. He stopped and turned to me.

"It's okay. Don't be afraid," he encouraged.

Glancing down the street, back toward my home, I

contemplated for a moment.

"I'm sorry, you can't go back home." He said. "He will expect you to go back to your friend."

Kiarra. My heart ached. *Wait, had he read my mind?*

"Come, before he sees us."

I took another deep breath before venturing forward into a forest I had never been in before; a forest I had many nightmares about in the past. Always the same nightmare of my parents running into the forest and leaving me behind.

Kieran turned and began running forward again. I raced after him, keeping pace with his steps as best I could.

It was almost the middle of the morning; the sun shafts were shining through the tree canopy. He led the way through, jumping over tree roots and fallen branches. The forest was oddly quiet; I couldn't hear any birds or insects.

I was relieved when he slowed to a walk after what felt like 10 minutes, as I was running out of breath. My lungs felt like they would explode. Having done minimal exercise lately, I was in no shape to be running a marathon. I gripped a nearby tree trunk; I was dizzy and thought I might collapse. As I looked over at him, he didn't seem to be laboured at all; he was breathing as if he had been relaxing in a chair. *Who were these people?*

"We're here." He finally broke the silence, staring ahead.

I looked around but saw nothing except for trees and shrubbery. Eyebrows raised, I stared at the tree trunks in confusion. My brain was waterlogged. I didn't have a clue what had just transpired or what would happen next. *Could I really trust this man I had just met? Did I actually have a choice? Or was I walking straight into a trap?*

Kieran glanced around. I watched him scout the trees. He faced the large tree directly in front of us and stretched out his right hand. Watching him intently out of the corner of my eye, I continued to hold onto the tree to keep my balance. He closed his eyes, and I observed as his entire face relaxed. How he could relax in a situation like this was beyond me.

Falling apart from the inside out, I crumpled, my knees buckling. I gripped the bark to steady myself. I had the urge to bolt, to find somewhere to hide where no one would ever find me. *How did this man know where to find me in the first place? Why was he after me? Who was he?* I would never find out the answers to my questions if I didn't see this through.

Kieran was so still for a moment that if he hadn't been standing, I would have thought he had fallen asleep. His fingers twitched as a swirling luminescent substance erupted out of them. I took a quick step backwards, letting go of the tree I was holding.

I stared as the purple swirly substance left his hand; it travelled a metre or so in front of him. Then it grew in front of my eyes as I gawked in astonishment. My eyes were dry from not blinking. I didn't know what to expect. The substance expanded into a swirling oval as I watched intently.

"What...is...*that*?" I questioned through stunned breaths.

"A portal," he replied casually.

"To where?" I choked out, finally blinking rapidly.

"Myrdreya."

Myr-*what*? *What was that? A place*? It had to be a place since portals take you to places...right?

He gestured with his hand toward the swirling essence he called a portal. I couldn't stop staring at it; it was mesmerising.

"You first," I said, shaking my head. *Did he think I would walk through an unknown portal before he, a stranger, did?*

"I must insist. I need to ensure you get into Myrdreya safely before I scout the area and follow you. Besides, the portal will close before you can enter if I go first."

I sighed at his words, but his argument made sense. For a reason I was yet to discover, someone was after me and wanted me dead. I could go home and possibly not wake up. Maybe that was a good thing. I wouldn't have to suffer any longer. I wouldn't have to live without Kiàrra.

Or I could walk through this portal and discover the truth.

The *truth*.

I wanted the truth. I needed the verity of everything to clarify that my life hadn't been a waste of time. A waste of the air I breathed.

Taking a deep breath, I stepped through the french-violet portal.

I had nothing else to lose. My parents had abandoned me, the love of my life had vanished, and my best friend had just been murdered. Everyone I had ever cared about was gone. The world I had once known wasn't the world I was now standing in.

Four

TRIXIE

*G*RAVITY DISAPPEARED. I was floating through thin air with colourful, swirly mist surrounding me. The colours were marbled with tiny flecks of silver; it was mesmerising. Time had slowed down again. I was moving, but everything around me shifted timelessly. Behind my ribs, my heart picked up its pace. *Did I need to do anything to get through this portal?*

A thousand thoughts rushed through my mind. *Did I make the right decision? Should I even be here? Why me? How are portals even real? Are they real? Am I just dreaming all of this? Will I wake up soon, back in my bed?* My mind was exploding with so many unanswered questions; the thoughts whirled around inside my head, making me dizzy.

When gravity reappeared a moment later, I fell. Closing my eyes tightly, I let out an ear-piercing scream. To my surprise, my feet touched the ground softly, and the feeling of falling was instantly gone.

The feeling of dirt between my toes was replaced with something very smooth—tiles, floorboards? I took a slow breath before opening my eyes, then I squinted in the blinding sunlight. Warmth flooded on my bare arms.

I blinked; then blinked a few times more. My jaw dropped open at the unbelievable sight standing before me. A rush of air escaped my lips, and my eyes widened. This had to be one endless dream. The air was so fresh here—impossibly fresh. I breathed in the wonderful, clean air as I stared ahead of me.

From the corner of my eye, I could see light illuminating behind me. I turned to stare at the portal, and Kieran appeared. I watched as the swirls in the purple portal faded, and then vanished entirely.

"Welcome to Myrdreya," Kieran announced as he stepped up beside me.

I glanced at Kieran momentarily before turning back to the magnificent view. I didn't know what to look at. Everything was stunning—and transparent. It was like I had floated into one of my dreams or walked into another world. *Wait, was I in another world?*

"I have to be dreaming." I muttered. Lightheaded, my head swimming in thoughts.

"If you're dreaming, you have one wild imagination," Kieran cackled.

Everywhere I looked, there was glass. The buildings, the trees, the ground—they were all glass. My body tensed as I stared down. I was standing on a semi-transparent platform; the smoothness under my bare feet was *glass. Where on Earth were we?* There was nothing below the glass except for fluffy white clouds. The platform we stood on would have been floating on its own if it wasn't for the bridge that connected it to the glass island.

"Please don't tell me you're afraid of heights?" He raised his eyebrows at my reaction.

"No, I'm not, thankfully," I said, staring at the clouds below. "Where are we?"

He followed my gaze. "I thought that would have been obvious."

Narrowing my eyes at him, I scowled. Sarcasm was the last thing I needed. I tucked my hair behind my ears as I waited for a serious answer.

"We are hidden from the rest of the world. Too high for planes to fly. There is a force field around us, which makes us invisible to anyone outside," he answered in a more serious tone.

"Incredible." I whispered.

"The wards also deter any outsiders away." He said.

"Outsiders?" I raised my eyebrows.

"Non-magic humans."

I shook my head in disbelief, "right."

Kieran stepped forward, moving with purpose across the bridge. I followed in step beside him, slightly uneasy about walking on glass, but the glass appeared to be thick — very thick.

"Why is it not windy? I would have thought it would be extremely windy up here?" I queried.

"The wards block out Mother Nature's elements," Kieran explained.

I raised my eyebrows. "Including rain?"

He nodded, a smile playing at the corner of his mouth.

"How were the wards made? How did this glass...island get up here?"

My mind was a whirlwind, exploding with questions. A world I never knew existed had just opened up to me. I didn't know what to think about my surroundings anymore. If this place was truly not a dream, then I didn't belong here.

"We store magic in the ward towers. The towers power Myrdreya to stay suspended in the air," he said.

"But...what if they fail?"

Feeling uneasy, I was now picturing the glass island falling from the sky and shattering into a million shards on the earth below.

He abruptly stopped walking and stared at me.

"Then we will fall out of the sky," he stated, watching my face.

"WHAT?" My eyes widened as I clasped my hand over my mouth.

"Don't worry, they have never failed in known history." He smirked, a laugh threatening to escape his lips.

Scowling, I dropped my hand.

I looked up at the towers, seeing five of them. Almost shaped like a stretched cone, they had intertwined swirling spikes crossing over each other at the top with a ball in the middle. The ball was glowing in an array of colours which were swirling and moving with each other. The towers were spaced evenly around the glass island — the tallest spires in Myrdreya. What a fascinating place. I closed my eyes and counted to 10 before reopening them.

I was still standing on the glass island.

"No matter how many times you close your eyes, you will reopen them and be in the exact same place," Kieran said smugly.

I rolled my eyes at him, but stayed silent.

Kieran smirked as he began walking again, leading the way through the city. The carvings on the walls of the buildings were remarkably unique. Every building was different; one had swirled designs, another had spikes, and another had leaves and vines. It must have taken days — no weeks, maybe months — to hand carve these beautiful designs.

Tears welled up in my eyes. If only Kiarra could have seen this, we could have explored this city together. I quickly blinked the tears away.

"Who hand-carved all these designs?"

Kieran laughed. "Hand-carved? It would take months to do that. They were created magically."

"Magic can do that?" My eyes widened with curiosity.

"Of course, magic is a beautiful thing. We don't just make portals and attack each other." He laughed again.

Unsure of what to make of this new city, I somehow felt warm inside. It was a renewed feeling; something I hadn't felt in months. Kieran's carefree jokes and laughter made this place feel welcoming instead of nerve-racking.

We strolled along paths that wound through buildings. I observed the glass my feet touched; it was smooth on the surface but looked like ice beneath. It was so thick beneath my feet; I couldn't see the clouds through it.

He led me toward a small tower in the middle of the floating island. Glass carvings of animals surrounded the base of the tower. We ascended the spiralling ramp up to the top; there was a sleek, fragile-looking railing around it. I wondered if anyone leaned on it, would it break and cause them to fall?

The view from here was amazing; I could see from one side of Myrdreya to the other. With almost a 360 degree view, it was the optimal location in the city.

At the top of the tower, a glass door stood ajar. A man

looked up from his desk and his face lit up with recognition. His hair was white and gelled into spikes. His eyes were emerald green. He was dressed similar to Kieran; however, he wore a long black jacket, which went down to his knees.

"Ah, Trixie," the man announced, "welcome."

I glanced at Kieran. *How did everyone know who I was when I did not know who they were?* Kieran held out a hand, allowing me to pass him. Stepping into the small round room, I took in my surroundings. There were photos on the frosted glass walls; pieces of paper with writing were stuck underneath. Squinting to see, I stepped closer to the nearest portrait, but Kieran walked up beside me, blocking my way.

"I am Demetri, leader of the Soul Council."

I tore my eyes from the photos and looked at the man, who was now standing in the middle of the room. Fingers braided together, his hands rested in front of him.

"We have been monitoring you since you were a child; since your parents left," Demetri said.

A tightening sensation grew in my chest, my heart skipping a beat.

"You knew my parents?" Curiosity was written all over my face.

"Yes," he answered, "they are gifted."

Gifted? I stared at him with an unspoken question, which, to my surprise, he answered.

"They are Soul Weavers. Your father can create

protection shields."

"Wow, I had no idea." My mouth hung open in disbelief.

My parents were magical; it was hard to believe as I had never seen them do magic. I thought over the words he had just said, and something dawned on me.

"Wait," I began slowly. "You just said *can*."

Demetri stared at me. His eyes flickered momentarily toward Kieran.

"My parents are alive, aren't they?" I questioned carefully.

He nodded, but stayed silent.

"Are they...here?" My heart skipped a beat as I spoke.

He glanced over at Kieran again. I looked over my shoulder and saw Kieran shift awkwardly from one foot to the other. Turning back to Demetri, I waited for his answer.

"No, your parents aren't here," he finally replied.

I shook my head. "Well, where are they?"

"This is already a lot for you to take in," Demetri stated, avoiding my question. "Why don't you get some rest while you adjust to your new life?"

My new life.

Demetri exchanged a wary glance with Kieran. I didn't miss the flash of questioning in their faces. They weren't telling me something. I narrowed my eyes at Demetri and clenched my jaw.

"My life has just been turned upside-down. I'm

confused, and I want answers, not rest!" I blurted out, my face feeling like it had drained of colour.

"I know you have many questions." Demetri's eyes flashed. "But you need to rest before you faint."

What an odd thing to say. I opened my mouth to argue, but then I understood. My head started spinning, and my vision became blurred. I wiped my forehead with the back of my hand; the latter was covered in a cold sweat. The room tilted sideways, and before I knew it, I was falling.

ALL I COULD see was black. My eyes twitched, and I realised they were closed. Slowly opening my eyes, I stared at the ceiling. It was glass, like everything else in Myrdreya. I could see the stars above. My lips parted as I stared at the twinkling specks in the night sky. Well, I definitely wasn't dreaming—this was *real*.

My head was a tempest; everything I knew was a lie. Magic was a myth—a lie. Detectives had told me my parents were most likely dead—a lie. *What else in my life had been a lie?* I didn't know what was real, and what wasn't anymore. *What was up, and what was down?* It was difficult to comprehend everything that had happened in the past 24 hours.

Still gazing at the night sky, I brushed a strand of hair off my face. Something moved beside me. I gasped, quickly sitting up.

"Sorry, I didn't mean to startle you." Kieran looked at me warily; he still wore the same black clothes. "How are you feeling?"

Somehow, his presence was comforting. His eyes twinkled in the soft moonlight shining through the transparent ceiling.

"Confused," I admitted, glancing around the dimly lit room.

My eyes drifted from the bookshelf and wardrobe on the left side of the room to the lounge chair opposite us on the right—all the furniture was made from glass. The bed frame, bedside tables, and the chair Kieran was sitting on were all beautifully crafted.

Feeling Kieran's eyes watching me as I examined the room, I turned back to him and asked, "Where am I now?"

"We're in your room," he replied.

"*My* room?"

He nodded. "Yes, you're welcome to live here now. After all, you are one of us."

"One of you?"

I swung my legs around to sit on the edge of the bed. It relieved me to know I was still wearing the same clothes. They had respected my privacy; I would have felt violated if someone had undressed me.

"You're gifted, like us," he stated, as if it was obvious.

I stared at him. "Gifted?"

He nodded again. "We are Soul Weavers."

"We are Soul—*what?*"

"Soul Weavers. In books, you would probably know us as warlocks."

"I am a warlock?" I was in disbelief. "But, I'm human."

"Yes, we're still human, but with gifts," he explained naturally.

I shook my head, closing my eyes. My head was whirling again. *What was going on? Was I gifted? Was I magical? Was I a warlock?* A memory flashed on the back of my eyelids. I realised something as my eyes snapped open.

"When that man mur—" I choked on my words. "Murdered Kiarra. Something happened."

"What?" He raised his eyebrows, sitting up straighter.

I took a breath. "It was like magic had come out of my fingers and hit him in the chest."

Kieran nodded in understanding. "You have never had that happen before?"

I shook my head.

"Soul Weavers are magical beings. When focused, we can channel our magic into doing great things—or bad things, in some cases. Dark Soul Weavers are what we call Soul Weavers who are using their magic for evil instead of good," Kieran explained.

"So, that man was a Dark Soul Weaver?"

"No. He was a Soul Hunter," Kieran stated.

I raised my eyebrows and blinked. "A Hunter?"

"Soul Hunters are humans with no magic who hunt Soul Weavers. You were lucky I was there to protect you."

I huffed. *So much information to take in; no wonder I had fainted.* I pinched my arm. Pain seared up my arm; I really wasn't dreaming.

"Satisfied you're awake?" Kieran teased, a smirk playing at the corner of his mouth.

I frowned at his comment, but ignored the question.

Pinching the bridge of my nose, I asked, "why were you there?"

"It was my mission to watch over you and come to your aid if danger should arise. Which it did."

"*I* was your mission?"

He nodded again. "We are trained to protect uneducated Soul Weavers from Soul Hunters. They believe we are an abomination—that we shouldn't exist."

"Uneducated?" I blinked.

He nodded. "Soul Weavers who don't know they are one."

Glaring at him in silence for a long moment, I chewed my tongue.

"You've been watching me and protecting my house for I don't know how long...yet, you didn't save Kiarra." My pulse quickened as anger boiled inside me.

Kieran shifted in the chair, momentarily taking his eyes off me before he spoke.

"I didn't get there in time." He hung his head, staring

down at his hands in his lap. "I'm sorry."

I shook my head. It was all too much, too fast. My parents were alive, which made their abandonment so much worse. I could do magic, which I never imagined could be real. And I was on a glass island floating above the clouds, which was shielded from anyone outside seeing.

Kieran went on, "When you have adjusted, we will start your training in Soul Weaver abilities. But, for now, you need to rest for a day or two and allow yourself to explore and accept your new life."

Kieran pushed himself off the chair and moved to leave.

"Wait," I called out to him.

He paused, turning back to me.

"What is this mark on my neck?" I asked, moving my hair to expose the semi-transparent white mark on my skin.

"It's the mark of a Soul Weaver. We all have it." He turned and showed me the same mark on his neck. "It is simply the mark of who we are. It appears on our skin when our magic grows within us. Without it, we are powerless."

With that, he smiled and exited my new room, leaving me alone. I didn't want to be alone. It meant my mind could wonder to places I didn't want it to.

If I hadn't taken that shower, or hadn't taken so long looking at myself in the mirror, I could have saved her.

Kiarra could still be alive. Her horrified face was plastered in my vision. Her wide, tearing eyes pleading at me for help. All I did was stand there and stare. He could have killed me, too.

Why didn't I know about this gift earlier? Why didn't I save her? I could have lunged at him and stopped him. He had no weapons, he only had his pure strength. She could have come to Myrdreya with me. *Can non-magical beings come to this world if invited?* This world. *Where is Myrdreya? Where am I?*

Looking around the glass room, tears overflowed my eyes again. Kiarra was gone, and it seemed this was my new life now.

Filling my lungs with air, I whispered to myself, "I can do this."

Five

"SO, WHAT'S SHE LIKE?" Jake asked as we strolled along the rocky roads in Kora.

"Who?" I replied as we rounded a corner in an alleyway.

Suited up in black, we were searching for clues for his girlfriend — or ex-girlfriend — in the small town of Kora located south and across the water from the Ice Mountain Isle. She liked the cold, so Jake thought we would start looking along the banks opposite the Isle.

Kora was the tiniest town I had ever been to. It seemed

everyone knew everyone here, so we were complete outsiders to everyone we passed. We got stared at—a lot. It didn't bother us, though; we were used to being gawked at in these small towns every time we left Myrdreya. It was the norm.

"Trixie." Jake raised his eyebrows.

I peered around another corner through the darkness. "Clueless."

"About what?"

"Our world, magic, *every*thing."

"Well, you can't blame her. She was raised in a human world and her parents left her." Jake stated.

"Yes, well, she's going to take a lot to train up." I said. "I may not be available to come on these adventures with you as much as I'd like."

Jake clapped me on the shoulder. "It's alright mate, I understand. Duty calls, right?"

I nodded as I sighed.

Most of the townsfolk had turned in for the night as soon as the sun had fully surpassed the horizon. We continued our walk in silence as we weaved along the roads and peered in through the windows of houses and buildings. We climbed up on top of some roofs to check the second floors and any attics that had windows.

Nothing.

"I don't think she's here." I said after an hour of scouting Kora.

Jake swallowed. I could see he was disappointed, but

agreed that she definitely wasn't here.

"Sorry bud, we'll have to try another town further north." I suggested. "Tyron?"

"Enough disappointment for today." He stated. "We'll check Tyron another day."

I really wanted to help him find her. He hasn't been the same since she left Myrdreya, when she left him. A darkness had come over him—not the type where he would turn into a Dark Soul Weaver—but he didn't have the spark of happiness he had whenever she was around. He was…empty.

Six

R EFRESHED.

For the first time in months, I awoke after a soundless sleep. Sitting in bed, I looked around the room—*my* room, Kieran had said. The walls were frosted, so no one could see in or out—that was a relief. With the sunlight peeping through the curtains, the genuine beauty of the crafted furniture glistened; plain, yet elegant.

Shoving back the silk, royal blue covers, I swung my feet over the edge of the mattress and climbed out of bed.

Crossing the room to the wardrobe, I pried the doors open and eyed the clothing. There was a mixture of styles, from elegant dresses to casual pant and top combinations. Spotting a simple pair of three-quarter black pants and an asymmetrical purple top, I checked the sizing. Perfect sizes for me. I shimmied out of my clothes and pulled on the new clothing.

I wandered over to the curtains and pushed them open, revealing clear glass doors that led out to a balcony. I gripped the handles and opened the doors, stepping out onto the suspended platform. How the mechanism worked in the locks was beyond my knowledge.

Leaning my palms on the balcony railing, I stared out over the glass city. I still couldn't believe it was all made from glass, or that it was levitating so high in the sky. It must weigh a billion tons. It was a glorious view; I loved the way the glass glistened like crystals as the morning sun touched it.

A soft knock sounded on my door, drawing my attention away from the city view. I could see a shadowed figure on the other side of the frosted glass. I hurried across the room and opened the door. Kieran stood waiting, his dark brown hair perfectly combed into spikes, except for the stray strand on his forehead.

He inclined his head. "Good morning, Trixie."

"Morning," I said.

I looked at the attire he was dressed in; it was much more casual than it had been yesterday. He wore dark denim jeans with a plain white shirt. He was extremely handsome in white; it complimented his dark-toned skin.

"I thought I would escort you around so you can see all of Myrdreya."

His smile was charming as he looked down at me. As I looked back up at him, I realised he was a whole head taller than me.

"Thank you, that sounds great."

I slipped on some white sandals from the shoe rack; they were my size. I didn't bother to question how they knew the sizes for my shoes and clothes — I wasn't sure I wanted to know. After all, they had been monitoring me for months; they probably watched for my sizes so they could properly accommodate me.

Following Kieran into the hallway, I closed the bedroom door behind me. There was no visible lock, so I shrugged and fell into step beside him; I had no possessions, so I had no need for a lock, anyway.

We strolled side by side through the small glass castle — as I called it. It wasn't really a castle, but it was the closest thing to it I had ever stepped foot in. Every wall was beautifully designed with creative patterns. I ran my fingertips along the closest wall, feeling the grooves that were carefully carved into it. Each curve looked like it had been deeply thought out.

"Our ancestors had created the city hundreds of years ago." Kieran said.

"The buildings and plants?"

"The ground you're standing on, all these buildings, trees, furniture...everything glass you see."

My jaw dropped.

"Everything?"

"Yes, everything."

"So, if something breaks, we can mend it—or someone here can mend it." I said.

"If it's broken and we have the pieces, yes, it can be mended. But if it's completely shattered or something is thrown off the edge...well, nothing can be done." Kieran replied.

"Couldn't it be...I don't know...re-conjured?" I asked.

He laughed. "Re-conjured? No—unfortunately, the blood line died out long ago. There is no one who can re-create such magic anymore."

We turned a corner, and I let my hand drop away from the wall. Kieran led me outside and along a pathway before turning toward a building. We walked under a magnificent archway lined with electric, swirling balls of energy. They were clearly made from glass, but somehow spun around like they were real. It was a rainbow archway resembling, I assumed, all the colours of the Soul Weavers' magic. Beyond the archway was a roofless, rectangular room. I stared in amazement at the activity in front of me.

Soul Weavers were spread around the room, wielding no weapons, yet they were sparring with one another. The nearest pair were casting and dodging each other's spells—at least I thought that *spell* was the correct terminology.

There was another pair in the middle of the room who seemed to be practising casting different spells. At the far end of the room, there was a trio. I watched them curiously. The man in the middle was shielding himself from a woman on one side, while casting another spell at the other—another man.

"Piggy in the middle?" I raised my eyebrows, feeling sorry for the man standing in the middle of the trio.

Kieran laughed. "It's not always a fair fight. They are practising two against one."

I nodded. "Right."

"This is the training ground." Kieran explained, "where we practice, obviously. The man in the middle is Nathan. He's known for his multitasking abilities," Kieran explained as Nathan spun away from the other man's spell.

The woman spun as she side-stepped and cast a pink energy ball around Nathan's aqua shield; it hit him in the shoulder before he could deflect it. The woman laughed.

The other man—whose magic was navy blue—had also thrown a spell at Nathan. Nathan had moved and narrowly missed the spell, while re-casting a shield to block the woman again.

"You're going to catch flies," Kieran joked.

I closed my mouth; I hadn't realised it was hanging open. Kieran laughed again. Narrowing my eyes, I scowled.

"Come, there's another room you will like." He turned and walked back through the archway.

We strolled across Myrdreya back toward the platform we had arrived on. He veered off to the left into another building; I stepped in behind him. This room was circular and full of portals around the wall edges. Each uniquely coloured portal swirled in diverse patterns.

"This is…"

"The portal room," I finished for him, staring.

He nodded; the corners of his eyes crinkled as he smirked.

"These are the general portals that are conjured at certain times of the day. If you want to go somewhere, you either use your own magic to conjure one or ask a portal keeper."

"I can conjure a portal?" My eyes enlarged.

"Of course—well, not yet. With training, you will be able to," Kieran said. "We can only portal out of Myrdreya from this room. We can portal in on the platform we arrived on yesterday or directly into this room."

I smiled as I looked around the room. The colours of the portals were reflecting off the glass walls, bouncing a rainbow around the room. It looked supernatural.

"Portals are monitored—for safety reasons. So we can see where others are going if we need to," he continued. "If someone is in trouble, and they recently took a portal from here, we can track them down. We also always know when a portal is opened into the city. That way, we can monitor who is coming and going."

I raised my eyebrows, my lips parting slightly.

"That's amazing," I mumbled as I stared at the mesmerising swirling pools of colour.

Seven

*L*EAVING TRIXIE BY HER BEDROOM door after exploring the city, I made my way back to my room. She enjoyed walking through Myrdreya with me — I enjoyed walking with her. I felt at ease around her. I wasn't sure why. A smile spread across my face; but it fell away as quickly as it came.

She really was clueless about our world, though. Zalindor had been my home since my parents sent me here and I knew an enormous amount about it before arriving. My mother had spent all her free time educating me before my father got home from work. Some days, I broke things or set them on fire; my mother always repaired them before he entered the house. If it hadn't been for her, I would have died that day along with them.

"Kieran." I heard someone call my name, pulling me abruptly out of my thoughts.

I stopped and turned to find Demetri striding up to me. His expression was stern.

"It's time for her training," he announced. "Begin tomorrow."

I nodded.

"We need to see what she can do." Demetri eyed me curiously. "Also, keep a watch on her. I'm not sure if we can trust her yet."

He turned and left me standing alone in the corridor. I watched as he turned the corner before ascending the stairs toward my room. He never trusted newcomers — not since Julianne and Jay had betrayed his trust. They had used him — learning all they could from him and then disappearing into the night. Trixie could do the same. I doubted it. She doesn't know enough to even want to betray us.

Entering my bedroom, I closed the door behind me. I crossed the room to my balcony and leaned against the open door frame, gazing out over Myrdreya.

Maybe Trixie wasn't as boring as she had appeared to be at her home. Perhaps she was just uninteresting when she was alone. I had been unsure about her for months; I thought she was a waste of my time. But maybe she was exactly what I needed in my life—a purpose for my existence. I had a feeling there was more to her than I could see.

A firm knock on the door startled me out of my thoughts. Crossing the length of the room, I gripped the door handle and wrenched it open.

"That time again?" I asked.

Jake stood in front of me, fully dressed in his battle attire.

"Well, I thought you might like to come with me and do some hunting." He smirked.

"Let me guess," I scratched my chin. "Hunting Soul Hunters?"

Jake threw his arms out wide and said sarcastically, "how did you know?"

I laughed.

"Clara has been looking for the Soul Hunter that killed Trixie's friend. She's got an address to go check out." Jake said.

"Great, let's go." I grabbed my jacket that I had thrown on the bed earlier today.

JAKE AND I discreetly crept down a dark alleyway in Katoomba, Blue Mountains, west out of Sydney. The same town that Trixie lived in.

The street lights bouncing off the cloud covered sky kept it from being pitch black, but down here it was nothing but darkness. The thundering and lightning wasn't comforting either. We pressed ourselves against a wall behind a large garbage bin.

"Where did you say Clara got this address from?" I whispered.

"Um, I didn't." Jake whispered back.

"And you didn't think to ask her?"

"We were interrupted by Demetri before she could tell me. She just said to come check it out."

I clenched my jaw, frowning. Narrowing my eyes, I peered down the alleyway toward a door at the far end. I pushed my senses forward, searching for anybody nearby. No one in the alleyway except us. *Well, I guess that could be a good thing, right?*

Jake frowned as he watched the door. It drizzled, slowly getting heavier. We glanced back toward the street, before creeping slowly forward. The door loomed ahead. It was a plain black door with a painted number on it—7.

When we reached the door, Jake stood watching the alleyway as I tried the lock. Of course, it was locked. I hadn't expected any less. Nothing my magic couldn't handle.

A moment later, I had the door unlocked, and we opened it a crack to peer in. There was a dull yellow light in the far corner. It was enough for us to see the entire room was empty. I pulled the door open, and we stepped inside, closing it behind us.

"Something's not right." He muttered.

"It's too quiet." I said.

Jake looked back at the door. "We got in here too easy."

We both looked around the vacant room. It had high ceilings, no furniture, no windows, and no other doors. The light in the corner was the only light source.

"There's nothing here." Jake said in a low voice, barely audible.

"Nothing but you two." A deep voice sounded from the doorway.

Jake and I spun toward the tall, muscular man. He stared at us with the dark eyes I remembered from the day I rescued Trixie.

"It's you." I said.

He eyed me over and said, "You're the one that got in my way."

"That's me!"

"You're going to regret that." The man spat, taking a step forward.

"No, I don't think I will." I said.

"But you might," Jake said, and he released a fireball toward the man.

He twisted to the side, jumped out of the path of it and grabbed a dagger out of a sheath on his belt. He lunged at Jake, his dagger soaring over his head, aiming for Jake's neck. I raised my hand, a fireball erupting from my fingers, and blasted the man off his feet and into the wall.

He rolled and pushed himself up from the ground as quickly as he had fallen. Jake pulled the dagger from his arm. Thankfully, it missed his neck.

The man's face twisted with anger. He gripped a new dagger from his belt, advancing towards us. I stepped in front of Jake, raising my hands. Purple electric fire sparked at my fingertips and grew into a shield, protecting us from the man's attack. He swiped at the shield, but couldn't penetrate it with the blade.

Jake threw a fireball through my shield and hit the man in the chest, knocking him backwards.

"Well done." A voice came from the door again.

Jake and I whirled toward the door, ready to attack the newcomer.

"Demetri?" I said, frowning at the white-haired man in the doorway.

Demetri stepped forward and a band of Soul Weavers followed in behind him. Two of them ceased the man by the shoulders. I released my shield and squared my shoulders.

"Who did you think gave you the address?" Demetri said.

"It was you," I said. "You gave it to Clara."

He inclined his head and turned to the other Soul Weavers. "Tie him up and make sure he's found by the local police with a full confession of the murder."

"How did you find the address?" Jake asked.

"I've been scouting to find the murderer, just as you have," Demetri said. "And now, it's over."

I stared into his cold eyes. He was hiding something.

Eight

TRIXIE

THUMP, THUMP, THUMP.

At first I thought it was still night, but then I saw the sun rising over the clouds on the horizon. As the sunlight hit the glass towers, rainbows of colour bounced around the room. It was like I was inside a colourful diamond—really magical.

"Trixie?" Kieran's voice came from the crack in the door as he opened it slowly.

"Com..on..en."

"Was that English?" Kieran's eyebrows raised high on

his forehead as he stepped in.

I groaned, shoving the covers back over my head.

"Come on, get dressed." He said, pulling the blanket off my face. "We've got work to do."

"At this time of the morning?" I mumbled.

"Wear something flexible and enclosed shoes." He stepped backwards out of my room.

I pushed myself up from the bed. "What are we doing?"

"Dress light," he called over his shoulder before he closed the door behind him.

I blinked, my shoulders growing slack. Crossing the room, I opened the wardrobe doors and searched for some light-weight clothes. After locating a pair of black leggings and an periwinkle-blue t-shirt, I closed the wardrobe and slipped the clothing on. A pair of white and black sneakers with socks resting on top was waiting for me in the shoe rack. Perfect.

I pulled on the socks and shoes and checked myself in the glossy glass wall; it wasn't very clear, but I could see that I looked half decent—except for my hair. I combed my fingers through it to break up the clumps of knotted hair to tidy it. Frowning, I searched around the room and spotted a brush on the beside table.

I dashed across the room and snatched up the brush, giving my hair a quick tidy up. After rechecking my reflection, I was satisfied.

Leaving my room, I closed the door behind me. Kieran

was patiently waiting in the corridor; his mouth twitched and curved into a smile. My heart hammered behind my rib cage. *Was I nervous? Why was it feeling like it would explode right out of my chest?*

He turned away from me and walked down the hallway; I followed silently behind him. He led me to the portal room; unlike yesterday, there were no active portals.

I inspected the circular room, biting my bottom lip. "Where are the portals?"

"They are shut down overnight if they aren't needed," he explained. "We need to conserve our powers, which is why they are only active for certain times during the day."

"What do you mean by conserve powers?"

"Well, if we use our powers repeatedly in a short amount of time, we weaken. That's why we have portal keepers who are allocated to open portals in the city. So the rest of us who venture outside of the city often can preserve our magic and strength," Kieran said.

It didn't even occur to me that magic had weaknesses. Nodding in understanding, I stepped forward, looking around the empty room.

"Today we're going to Elvanor Forest." Kieran stepped up beside me.

"Are you going to open a portal?"

A moment later, my question was answered. A woman dressed in a dark red trench coat with black pants strode into the portal room and positioned her hand in front of her. Closing her eyes, swirls of crimson escaped her fingertips as a portal formed on the right side of the room.

"Thank you, Delaras." Kieran bowed his head to the woman, and she stepped aside.

The woman looked familiar, but I couldn't figure out why. She had bright red hair, just like the colour of her magic and her coat. Delaras glanced at me for a moment, her brown eyes unreadable. I quickly adverted my eyes.

"We will go through together." The sound of Kieran's voice drew my attention back to him.

He stepped in front of the swirling crimson portal and held out his hand to me. I walked forward and took his hand—my heart skipping a beat. We stood hand in hand, our fingers interlocked, in front of the portal.

My stomach somersaulted as we stepped toward the swirling oval. A mix of emotions was pouring throughout my body; I couldn't tell what exactly I was feeling. *Scared to go through the portal? Anxious that I was holding the hand of a handsome man?*

We stepped forward in unison.

The gravity shifted as we entered the portal. Everything slowed, and I closed my eyelids. Seconds later, our feet were back on the ground; it felt much faster than the first portal I had travelled through to get to Myrdreya.

I opened my eyes; we were standing in a lush green forest. A warm breeze touched my cheeks and whisked my hair out behind me. Glancing up at Kieran, I saw his eyes skimming the trees in the dim light. He was looking for danger. The light wind rustled the leaves in the thick tree canopy. Birds whistled and insects buzzed. That was all I could hear.

I hadn't realised we were still holding hands until he began walking, and he released my hand. My heart skipped another beat.

"Where are we going?" I trudged through the forest after him.

It had recently rained. The dirt had turned to slushy mud, and the leaves on the trees were dripping water. When I was a child, I had been terrified of the forest— afraid that I wouldn't be able to escape. Somehow, I felt safe with Kieran alongside me. He was my guardian, and I knew I was safe as long as he was with me.

"Not far. The forest is great for training the senses," Kieran answered as he jumped effortlessly over a moss-covered log.

I climbed over the fallen tree, supporting myself with both hands. The last thing I wanted was to slip arse over tits and face-plant in front of Kieran.

"Senses?" I queried, dusting the dirt off my hands on my pants.

He nodded. "Your hearing and sight."

"There's nothing wrong with my senses," I said, my eyebrows pulling together.

He chuckled and turned to face me. I almost walked straight into him. My breath drew in sharply, and I immediately took a step backwards.

"We are going to heighten them." The corner of his mouth curled up.

For a moment, I was enticed by the handsome face looking at me and the stubborn strand of hair dangling over his forehead—it gave him character; I thought. I watched as his lips twitched, and his smile broadened. My breath caught in my throat when I realised he was watching me.

I glanced away, pretending I hadn't been staring at him. "So, how do we heighten them?"

"Close your eyes." He whispered.

I stared at him for a moment. *Why did he have to be so attractive?* The smooth skin on his face, perfectly shaped lips, and sparkling almond-shaped eyes. Even if I wanted to, I couldn't bring myself to deny it.

He stepped closer. "It's okay, Trix."

I blinked, startled by the nickname I had only heard Levi call me. Somehow, it sounded sensual hearing it come from Kieran's lips.

"You can trust me."

I nodded in submission. *How could I not?* Closing my eyes, I listened for his voice.

"Now, I want you to clear your mind." The words were almost a whisper. "Listen to the leaves rustling, the morning birds singing, and the creatures scurrying across the vegetation. Smell the dirt, the bark, and the water in the air."

I let my mind be free of thoughts of my parents, my

best friend, my ex-boyfriend, and the overwhelming new world that had opened up to me. I forced myself to hear the forest—really hear it for what it was.

A non-forest smell hit my nostrils; it smelt like...like perfume. I realised it was Kieran's cologne; a blend of cedarwood, lavender and a hint of patchouli. Oh my, he smelt good. My heart stopped for a moment when his hands rested upon my shoulders. I knew he was standing directly in front of me because his fingertips were curled onto my back, and I could feel his breath on my face.

"Concentrate," he whispered. "Feel the forest."

I couldn't feel anything around me except for his close presence. I was nervous with him so close. *How was I supposed to focus on anything except how damn good he smelt?*

As if he sensed he was distracting me, he released me. I didn't know whether I should be relieved or disappointed. I took a deep breath to refocus on the forest.

"Hear the birds in the trees. Listen to them, twittering and playing in the sunlight," he continued.

My brows pulled in. *What birds? I couldn't hear any bir—oh!* I suddenly heard twittering birds. It was like I could see what they were doing on the back of my eyelids. They jumped from tree branch to tree branch. I opened my eyes and looked into the trees to see the birds, but I could only see empty branches.

"But I saw..." I trailed off as I searched the surrounding trees, confused.

"What did you see?" Kieran asked, curiously

following my eyes into the trees.

"The birds you mentioned. They were playing and jumping around."

He nodded and grinned. "Well done."

I didn't understand. There were no birds nearby. I stared at him with a silent question.

"You saw birds that are one hundred metres away."

My jaw dropped. "No...way."

"In that direction." He pointed behind me.

I didn't know why I did it, but I walked to the nearest tree and touched it. Placing my palm hard against it, the damp bark was rough under my fingers. I turned back to Kieran; he was watching me curiously. He pressed his lips together like he was holding in laughter; the corners of his mouth twitching.

"Are we in some kind of simulation?" I asked, cocking my head to the side.

"No, of course not." He laughed, not being able to hold it in any longer. "We train in the real world."

I glanced around at the forest—it certainly looked real, and the tree my palm touched felt real. Taking another breath, blushing from embarrassment, I closed my eyes once more. I let my senses control me.

I listened to the leaves crunching and the tree trunks creaking. The wind blew my hair, and I could smell fresh water. I followed the scent of the water through the forest and found a running creek. Following the creek along its banks, there was a sound of splashing. I zoned in on the splashing, and I could hear gulping. *An animal drinking water?*

I focused heavily on the animal. I couldn't see it as clearly behind my eyelids as I had with the birds, but I could hear its movements. The figure was blurred and dark, like a shadow. It stopped drinking and stood up. Then it spoke—not an animal.

I gasped, and my eyes shot wide open. "A person!"

Kieran's eyes widened before he stared off into the distance. His face was blank. After a few seconds, he blinked and leapt forward, grabbing my hand.

"Soul Hunters," he whispered urgently.

He stretched out his free hand and closed his eyes. I watched his beautiful face as his features partly relaxed. Swirling magic erupted from his hand and formed the same portal he had summoned when we first met. A stick broke nearby, and Kieran didn't hesitate—he wrapped his arm around my waist, pulling me close, then into the purple portal with him.

Nine

OUR FEET TOUCHED DOWN ON the same platform I had arrived on two days prior. Glancing over my shoulder, I saw the portal fade and disappear. I stared at the vacancy of the portal. The forest had seemed so surreal; if it hadn't been real, Kieran wouldn't have acted that way.

"I must report to Demetri." Kieran's concerned voice brought my attention back to him. "Soul Hunters haven't been seen in Elvanor Forest for hundreds of years."

I nodded, unsure of what to say. Kieran left me

standing on the platform as he hurried away. I watched as he disappeared around a corner. I was fascinated by how the walls were made from glass, but I couldn't see much through them.

I stared at the place he disappeared. He hurried away so quickly that he hadn't given me a chance to question him. No one would dash away that swiftly without having a secret; he was hiding something. I was sure of it.

Not knowing what to do with myself, I wandered through Myrdreya for the next hour. I passed several other Soul Weavers as I strolled along the paths inspecting the unique buildings. I was still amazed by the carvings on the walls and doors. The windows were crystal clear, but the edges were framed like old-fashioned photo-frames. *How had Myrdreya been built? Had someone decide to just start carving out of a massive piece of glass and use magic to suspend it into the air out of reach of prying eyes?*

Strolling along the glass path back toward my room, I heard my name being called.

"Trixie." A woman's voice sounded from the right.

I looked over and stopped walking. Delaras, the woman from the portal room, was striding over to me.

"I wasn't sure if you would be one of us," she said. "Your parents didn't think you had any magic."

I frowned. Had *she recognised me as well?*

She stopped in front of me as I questioned, "What do you mean?"

"I knew you as a child," she stated, not elaborating.

Red hair, dark brown eyes…those red pursed lips. Surprise replaced my confusion.

"Delaras…" I repeated her name in a low mutter.

A wicked grin spread across her face.

"You were my next-door neighbour," I announced louder than I had anticipated.

Delaras nodded, her short crimson hair bobbing with the movement.

"Delaras," a stern voice behind her said, "you didn't mention that you knew Trixie."

Delaras and I both glanced over to see Kieran standing there. He had the same concern on his face now as when he had left me earlier.

She glanced at me before turning back to Kieran. "I didn't think it mattered."

"Of course it matters. You could have had information for us when we were trying to locate her." Kieran stared at her, eyes piercing.

"I knew nothing of her whereabouts." Delaras clenched her jaw.

Kieran stared at my face for a moment, as if trying to read it. Feeling awkward, I held onto my arms, yet it wasn't even slightly cold. The force field around Myrdreya must keep out the cold temperature of winter — or the warmth of summer. I wasn't sure where in the sky we were.

"Thank you, Delaras," he said dismissively. "I will escort Trixie from here."

His words were final. Delaras' face was hard. She glanced at me briefly before departing. I stared back at Kieran, watching his worried features. His eyes were on the back of Delaras' head.

He waited until Delaras was out of sight before he spoke again. "How do you know her?"

"She was my next-door neighbour."

He waved away my answer, his eyes boring into mine. "I know that, but it sounded like she was more than just a neighbour."

"Yes, well, she came over to my parent's house every few days for about a month before..." I trailed off.

"Before what?" He cocked his head to the side.

I stared at the space between us. A tightening in my chest, making it difficult to breathe.

"Before my parents abandoned...me." I choked.

He took a couple of steps forward, stopping directly in front of me. "I know it must be a painful memory, but if you can remember anything unusual about that month, you need to tell me."

My eyes unfocused as I relived the memories in my mind—Delaras knocking on the front door and my parents sending me to my bedroom every time she did. I vaguely heard my name being called as I remembered the day when I had come out to find my house empty. Gone. My parents were gone.

"...Trixie!" Kieran waved a hand in my face, and I clicked back to reality.

I realised it had been him calling my name.

"S-sorry," I stuttered, blinking my eyes rapidly to stop the tears.

He brought a hand up to my cheek and wiped away a tear. I looked up into his eyes. Realising how close he was standing to me, my breath caught in my throat. My heart rate picked up speed.

"Are you okay?" he asked, his voice much calmer, but his stunning eyes clear with concern.

"I..." I shifted nervously, and my knee hit his. I stepped backwards. "Sorry."

Not paying the slightest attention to our contact, Kieran glanced around the surrounding area. Following his eyes, I saw a few bystanders chatting amongst themselves, paying no attention to us.

"Let's go somewhere more private. Perhaps you will be more comfortable to talk?"

I nodded hesitantly. I wasn't sure I actually wanted to talk. Bile crept up, and I swallowed, forcing it back down.

Kieran grasped my hand and led me through Myrdreya. I let him intertwine his fingers with mine. It felt almost natural. Looking out of the corner of my eye, I glanced at the side of his face. His jawline was soft and relaxed.

Just when I thought we were going back to my room, he turned up a flight of stairs and travelled along another corridor. At the end of the hallway, we stopped in front of a door. My brows furrowed as he pushed it open without knocking. He released my hand as he led me into the room; it was like mine. He ducked behind me, closing the door. My eyes wandered around the room; there was no one else here.

He headed for the comfortable-looking lounge chair on the opposite side of the room; I didn't have such a lounge chair in my place. He gestured for me to join him as he seated himself. I sauntered across the room and sat down beside him.

"Trixie, you don't need to be afraid." Kieran spoke in a hushed manner; his voice was angelic. "We are here to help you. You may know information vital to saving Soul Weavers."

My eyes closed. Saving Soul Weavers. *Were we dying out?*

"Trix...you can trust me." His voice was even softer than before. The sound of my nickname on his lips was so soothing that I wanted to melt into his arms.

I opened my eyes and took a breath. "A month before my parents disappeared, Delaras often visited our house. I would be sent to my bedroom and told not to come out."

I glanced over at Kieran; he listened intently as I continued, "I was curious, so I would sneak down and try to listen. I didn't hear much; they would lock themselves in the study."

"So, what *did* you hear?" Kieran questioned.

"They seemed to be planning something." I looked directly into his eyes as I pulled at my fingers. "I couldn't hear what, though."

He nodded, frowning slightly.

"I came down one night, and they were gone. My parents had vanished." Tears welled up in my eyes as my voice broke. "I haven't seen or heard from them since."

Kieran looked at me with concern. His body twisted toward me.

"I'm sorry you had to go through that." His voice was barely a whisper.

"I ended up in an orphanage until I turned 16. Then I got a job and moved into my own home," I said, placing my hands flat on my lap.

Kieran stayed silent for a long while. I looked at him, but his expression was unreadable.

"Anything else you remember?" he asked.

I shook my head.

"Thank you, Trix. I know how hard that must have been for you. But it was important." Kieran placed his soft hand on mine.

A weak smile curled at my lips as I looked into his eyes. His touch was soothing.

"I want you to know that you can talk to me about anything," he whispered, his hand still on mine.

"Thank you." I nodded.

After a moment, he released my hand and stood up. "I need to go back and speak with Demetri. Tomorrow morning, we will begin your endurance training. Why don't you go get some rest for the rest of the afternoon?"

Saying nothing, I just nodded again.

"Can you find your way back to your room?"

"Yes, I think so," I replied. "Whose room are we in, anyway?"

He smiled. "Mine."

Oh, he had taken me back to his room? I watched as he turned and left the room, closing the door behind him. Wow...he must have trusted me enough to leave me alone in his bedroom. *Was I being too paranoid? Maybe he wasn't hiding anything?*

Looking around his bedroom, I noticed how tidy it was. His shoes were lined up on the rack, his clothes hung on hooks, and his bed was made like a hotel bed.

A photo-frame sat on the bedside table. Pushing myself off the lounge chair, I strolled over to it. A photo of a woman and a man who looked about the age my parents would be stared back at me. Kieran's nose was the same as the man's, and he had the woman's eye and hair colour. His parents. I smiled.

⋙⦿⋘

AFTER FINDING MY way back to my room, I collapsed on my bed—slumping onto the light blue decorative cushions.

My parents had disappeared and left me all alone. *What parent would do that to their child?* That was when my depression had started.

I was a young teen who was still learning to budget, and they had abandoned me. The orphanage had somehow been notified and came to collect me the next day. Detectives visited me a few times over the following months; they couldn't tell me if my parents had died, disappeared, or runoff. Their bodies were never found.

I lived in the orphanage for the next few years until I came of age and could live on my own—as long as I had a job. So I set out to find a job and an apartment, so I could get out of there. They had treated me well at the orphanage, but I had been miserable there. Every day was a reminder of my parents' abandonment.

Within weeks, I found employment at a cafeteria, and I found housing for teenagers like me—children with no parents or support. I thought having my own place would improve my life, but I never felt more lonely and trapped.

Leaving the house to go for a walk was such an effort that I could never bring myself to do it—that was until I saw a handsome black-haired man jogging past my house one morning. I saw him every morning, around the same time. I pretended to be collecting the mail one day as he jogged past. He glanced over at me and smiled. My heart skipped a beat. Each morning, our friendship grew until we grew so close that we locked lips.

With Levi in my life, I had been slowly healing from the trauma of my abandonment. He had been putting my heart back together again—piece by piece. But it never completely healed. The sorrow of my parents leaving haunted me every day.

Levi's abandonment was just as bad as my parents'. My heart shattered into a million pieces when he left my house that day and disappeared. He left me to melt away, to drown in my misery once again.

Then everything had changed again. My life had been such a whirlwind already. Within a few hours, a man had murdered my best friend, Kieran had rescued me, and I found out that my parents were alive.

I didn't know how much more I could take. One thing I knew, and was afraid of, was that Kieran made me feel safe. I trusted him.

Ten

*K*IERAN COLLECTED ME FROM MY room soon after breakfast had been delivered the next day. I gulped down the last mouthful of apple juice and slipped into the white and black sneakers I had worn to the forest. We didn't go to the portal room this time; he lead me to another building opposite. It was the gym—or exercise room—I wasn't sure what they called it here.

"First, you need to learn to control your breathing on the endurance machine." Kieran gestured toward the machine in the far corner of the room.

We crossed the room.

"Um, is that safe?" I raised my eyebrows.

"Of course," his mouth turned up in a quirky smile.

Hesitantly, I stepped onto the flat surface of the machine. It looked like a treadmill in gymnasiums—kind of. The walking ramp was clear and smooth. *Was I going to fall through this thing? Or slip arse over and embarrass myself?*

Kieran started the machine, and I grabbed onto the rails for support. It began slowly and accelerated. My walking pace quickly turned into a run, and I was losing my breath fast. I looked down at my feet; the clear panel was moving, but I had no idea how.

"Focus on your breathing," Kieran hushed beside me.

Well, what else was I supposed to do?

"Breath in…and out…deeply and slowly."

I took my eyes off the walking panel and looked straight ahead. My hair was freely bobbing up and down on my back with each step I took.

After what only felt like ten minutes, I could feel myself getting dizzy—and fast. My heart was pounding, and my focus was getting blurred. I heard Kieran calling my name as my legs buckled beneath me. My eyes rolled into the back of my head and all I saw was darkness.

OPENING MY EYES, I stared at the transparent ceiling. I was lying on my bed, still wearing shoes. *Not again.*

I heaved a sigh. "Shit."

"Hello to you too." A voice I recognised instantly sounded next to me.

I bolted upright. Heat radiated from my cheeks — a burning sensation. *Crap!* Just when I thought it couldn't be more embarrassing, I had to swear in front of him.

"How are you feeling?" Kieran was sitting in a chair beside me, a smirk playing at the corner of his mouth.

I shrugged. "I'm all right."

Nodding, he pushed himself up from the chair and said, "I need to speak to Demetri. I just wanted to wait until you came back to consciousness."

I smiled inwardly. *Why was he so caring?*

"Take the rest of the day off to recover." He eyed over me. "You need it."

Exiting my room, he closed the door, leaving me alone. I stared at the door where he had been a moment before.

Without a second thought, I jumped off the bed and headed out into the hallway. *What did he need to speak to Demetri about? He seemed to always report to him.* Curiosity got the better of me.

Kieran was just turning the corner at the end of the corridor. Closing my bedroom door quietly, I followed him as discreetly as I could. He hurried through the city, and I hid behind walls and trees as I continued trailing him, keeping my distance.

Looking around me, I quickly scouted the nearby buildings—no one was in sight. I walked imperceptibly up the ramp; spiralling my way up the tower to Demetri's headquarters.

Peering around the last corner, I saw Kieran step inside. I crept up the remaining length of the ramp, keeping hidden against the curved wall. Once I was certain he was well inside, I leant closer.

The sun was on the opposite side of the tower, so I pressed my back against the glass wall; it was thick and frosted. I didn't think they would see my shadow through it. Kieran had left the door open a small crack, and I strained to listen to their conversation.

"… it was Julienne and Jay in the forest, not Soul Hunters." Kieran's voice said.

I swallowed at the sound of my parents' names, my stomach churning. I frowned; Kieran had told me the noise was from Soul Hunters. He had lied to me. *Why? How could he be so caring and then lie?* I *trusted* him. My heart pounded against my rib cage.

Many emotions swept over my body—anger, disappointment, betrayal, sadness. I didn't know how I should have been feeling. I had felt safe with him, trusted him, but he had lied to me.

"You didn't mention that yesterday." A deep voice rumbled through the thick glass; I recognised Demetri's voice.

"I know. I wasn't certain."

"And what makes you so certain now?" Demetri asked.

"My dream last night...it was them," Kieran said.

There was silence for a long moment. I swallowed, staring at the crack in the door. My breathing was heavy.

Demetri sighed. "How did they know Trixie was there?"

"Delaras." I heard Kieran state sternly.

"And your reasoning?" Demetri returned bluntly.

"She was the only one who knew we had gone to Elvanor Forest; she had opened the portal for us."

My heart hammered faster, harder. I stepped closer to the door. My skin was prickling with goosebumps, but not from being cold.

"We should tell her," Kieran stated.

"Not yet," Demetri said firmly. "She is still trying to comprehend her new life without adding the truth about her parents."

"But she deserves to know!" Kieran argued.

My breathing quickened, and my heart felt like it would leap out of my chest. *What truth did they speak of?*

Demetri's voice was final. "Not now."

I heard Kieran sigh, and the door suddenly swung open. I jumped backwards. He stepped out and stared at my pained face.

"Too late," Kieran called out to Demetri, not taking his eyes from mine.

He didn't seem surprised at all to see me there, almost

as though he had expected it.

Demetri's footsteps could be heard as he came toward the door. He peered around the doorframe.

"Trixie." He stared at me.

I glanced at Demetri for only a moment before looking back at Kieran. Feeling nauseous, I turned and hurried away.

"Trixie—WAIT!" Kieran yelled out.

Ignoring his desperate calls. I ran as fast as my legs would carry me, down the tower and across the city. Weaving through the glass buildings, I tried to lose him. A hand caught me by my forearm and spun my body around. *Of course, he was too fast for me.* My body slammed into him, and he held me tightly against him.

I fought against him, punching my hands against his chest. "Let...me...go!"

"Trix," he said, "let me explain."

"I don't want to hear your excu—" My words were stifled as Kieran pressed his lips on mine.

I froze; my body tensed. I could smell his cologne radiating off him. *Why did he have to smell so damn good all the time?* His lips were urgent on mine.

Kieran pulled away, and I stared up at him. I had not expected that, and I didn't know how I felt about it. My lips were slightly parted, but I said nothing. A thousand thoughts whirled in my head as I stared into his brown eyes.

"Now that you're calm," Kieran whispered, "please,

let me explain."

Closing my mouth, I glanced around the surrounding area. There was no one in sight; I was thankful no one had seen that. Nodding, I gave in. He relaxed his grip on me, but still held me very close. His hips were against mine, and I was very aware of the bumps and crevices on his body.

"I'm sorry you had to find out that way. I wanted to tell you, but Demetri forbid it," Kieran explained, looking into my eyes.

His brown eyes were so stunning, I couldn't help but stare back. They had a little silver in them; if I hadn't known better, I would have thought he was wearing contact lenses. But there was definitely no rim of contact lens to be seen. He was mesmerising. His dark brown hair complimented his eyes, making them stand out as if they were glowing.

"I knew you had followed me," he said. "Senses, remember?"

My face flushed. I felt stupid for not realising. Of course he would know.

"Your parents abandoned you," he continued.

"Tell me something I don't know," I mumbled, looking away.

His fingers found my chin and gently pulled my face to look at him again. "They left to become Dark Soul Weavers."

My face was blank; I wondered if he could read the

anxiety on it. My breathing was heavy.

"They aren't good people, Trix," he said in a whisper, "I lied to you about the people in the forest being Soul Hunters for a good reason."

"They were my *parents*," I stated.

Kieran nodded, still softly holding my chin.

"Yes, they were your parents. I couldn't let you see them before you understood who they are," he explained.

Shifting awkwardly, with his body still against me, I sighed and ground my teeth.

"We don't know exactly what they are capable of. But we know they are after you." He dropped a hand away from my waist and massaged the back of his neck. "It's why I was watching you — for months."

Throat suddenly feeling dry, I swallowed to get it moist again.

"For months?"

"Yes." He let go of my chin, then glanced away, his cheeks blushing.

I hadn't seen him blush before; I allowed myself to smile at him. His eyes came back to mine and his lips slightly parted. His jawline was perfectly aligned. He leaned in toward me. My heart pounded, but I couldn't move. He lingered close to my face, giving me time to escape if I wanted to. But I couldn't take my eyes away from him. He pressed his mouth against mine again, this time a lot softer. I closed my eyes and leaned into him. His arms wrapped around me, one hand on my lower back.

A lump appeared in my throat. I pulled away, pushing him away from me. He let me break free this time, staring at me.

"I'm sorry, I-I can't." That was all I said before turning and dashing away from him as fast as my feet could master. I didn't dare look back.

꙰꙰ ◉ ꙰꙰

LEANING AGAINST THE railing on my bedroom balcony, I thought about the day's events. My parents were Soul Weavers, and they had abandoned me to join the dark side.

Tears rolled down my cheeks; it was worse knowing why my parents had abandoned me. I suddenly wished I hadn't followed Kieran and learnt what he hadn't told me. But it was too late. I knew the heartbreaking truth now and had to work out how to deal with it.

How was I going to deal with it? I hastily wiped away my tears. My sadness quickly turned to anger. I was furious that my parents could do such a thing to their child—to me. They had shown me so much love when I was young, but then it dissipated when they started meeting with Delaras.

Delaras—it was all her fault. I ground my teeth together. She took my loving parents away from me, and now she was pretending she was innocent. I knew better, and I knew Kieran did, too.

I went for a night stroll to clear my head. The last thing I wanted to do was something I would regret. I didn't know exactly what that would entail, but I knew it would have something to do with letting all my anger out on Delaras.

Myrdreya was beautiful at night. No, it was stunning. The glass walls of the buildings were lit up with coloured lights; it made the glass look like coloured ice. I made my way across the island, passing very few people along the way.

Trying not to think about how angry I was, I focused on the beauty of the city instead. I found a beautiful fountain in the heart of Myrdreya. There was a garden surrounding it and a white bench seat. Sighing, I sat and looked up.

Gazing up at the glistening stars through the shield, I wondered what Levi would be doing. *Did he have a new girlfriend? Was he thinking about me? What would he think of my new found magic?*

Then my thoughts changed to Kieran. He had kissed me—*twice*. I didn't know how to feel about it; I was so hung up on Levi that I hadn't thought about being with anyone else. The way Kieran looked at me with his stunning silvery-brown eyes had me melting. The thought of his soft hands on my body made me tingle all over. His soft lips…

"Trix?"

I jumped off the bench seat at the sound of my name.

Kieran stood nearby but seemed to keep his distance.

"Sorry, I didn't mean to startle you," he said.

I sighed. "It's okay, I was just..." I thought back to what I was thinking about. "I was just admiring the night sky."

Kieran looked up. "Yes, it is wonderful at night."

I nodded.

"And there's no street lights here to shut out the view." He said.

He was trying to lighten the mood. I sat back down on the seat and continued watching the stars. I saw movement beside me; Kieran had seated himself next to me. Fiddling with a button on my pants pocket, I sat in silence, keeping my eyes on the sky.

"I went to your room, but you weren't there. I was afraid you had left. But someone said they had seen you walking this way." He whispered.

"I needed to clear my head," I replied.

"I just wanted to make sure you were all right. The truth about your parents must have been a shock." Kieran stated.

I breathed heavily, but stayed silent. I came out here to clear my head, not to talk about my parents.

"When you are ready to know more, let me know, and I will tell you anything you want to know," he said.

Unable to form words, I continued staring up at the twinkling stars in the night sky. I was thankful that he hadn't mentioned our kisses. He must have sensed I wanted to be alone, as he stood and walked away without another word.

Eleven

S ITTING ON THE EDGE OF my bed, I couldn't get Trixie off my mind.

I had kissed her twice, but she had bolted away. She clearly hadn't wanted to see me tonight. *Had I read her wrong? Maybe she doesn't like me that way?* She had been staring at me when we were in the forest, though.

Her platinum blonde hair hung in waves around her shoulders. She had beautiful, smooth skin. Surprising. She hadn't exactly been looking after herself for at least a few months — that I had seen, anyway.

Hammering on my door pulled me out of my speculations. I hastily crossed the room and opened the door.

"Clara?" I jolted. "You would think I would get used to your crazy hair colours."

She scowled at me, her eyes unblinking.

"Bright pink, really?" I teased.

She pursed her lips. "Better than having the same hair-do *every* day like *you*."

I poked my tongue out at her.

"On a more serious note, we have tracked them," Clara replied. "It's time. I asked Jake, on your behalf, to continue Trixie's training in your absence. I hope that is okay?"

"Of course, thank you." I sighed.

Clara waited outside for me as I dressed in my fighting gear and accompanied her to the portal room.

"Are you okay? You seem tense." Clara looked at me out of the corner of her eye.

"Yes, I'm fine," I lied. "We've been searching for clues for years, would be good to actually find something for a change."

"Agreed." Clara said as we entered the portal room.

I halted in the doorway when I looked up and saw Delaras. She eyed me for only a moment, her expression unchanging, before opening a portal for us.

I stepped forward cautiously. I didn't trust her. *Did she lead us on this track? Is she trying to throw us off their trail?*

Demetri has to know there's something not right about her.

"Thank you, Delaras," Clara chirped before turning to me. "Ready?"

I nodded slowly, watching Delaras. She smiled at me pleasantly, faking that she couldn't sense my apprehension, no doubt.

Clara went through the portal first. Taking my eyes off Delaras, I followed immediately after.

We landed in a grass clearing, surrounded by oak and elm trees. They were lushly green and spaced apart enough that the moonlight could shine through, lighting up the forest floor.

"Where are we?" I asked.

Clara scouted the area with her eyes. "Forluca Forest."

I raised my eyebrows. Forluca forest, a small cover of trees not even named on maps, south-east of Tyron. *This was going to be a waste.*

She pursed her lips. "I can't sense anyone."

"Of course not," I muttered as I, too, pushed out my senses to skim the forest.

I was not in the least bit surprised. There were plenty of birds and a few fawns, but there weren't any people.

Clara turned to me. "What was that about, back in the portal room with Delaras?"

I sighed. "I don't trust her."

She stared at me questioningly, expecting me to continue.

I exhaled. "I think she's in league with the J's."

Clara's mouth opened slightly as she considered my words. Her eyebrows pulled in.

"Why do you think she has anything to do with Julianne and Jay?"

"I have a bad feeling about her. She was the only one who knew Trixie, and I was going to Elvanor Forest for training," I stated. "I think she told them where Trixie would be."

"That's a serious accusation," Clara retorted, eyes narrowing slightly.

I nodded, swallowing.

"There's definitely no one here," Clara said, disappointed.

I shook my head. "No. There's no scent of people at all...well, maybe only you."

Clara snorted. "Oh, because I smell worse than your stench?"

"I showered this morning."

"And I didn't?"

"Well, your hair is bright pink. I would think you wouldn't want to get it wet." I said sarcastically.

She rolled her eyes.

"Come on, let's explore the territory to be sure," Clara said as she pushed forward through the forest.

Sighing, I reluctantly followed.

Twelve

I EXPECTED KIERAN TO KNOCK on my door to wake me for more training; however, it was the sun shining through my eyelids that woke me. I glanced around my room. There was no trace of him being here this morning. Climbing out of bed, I walked onto the balcony. The sun was already high in the sky. I blinked. *Was it the middle of the morning already?*

I leant on the railing. *Where was Kieran today?* It was odd he hadn't come to collect me this morning for more training. *Was he avoiding me because of yesterday's events?*

My mind started wandering.

He had held me so delicately when he kissed me the second time. I'm not that breakable, surely. I frowned at myself. My tongue traced my lower lip. His lips had pressed against mine like they were shaped to be together. The minty taste from his mouth had lingered on my lips for at least half an hour afterwards.

A loud knock on my door made me jump out of my thoughts. I shook my head, pushing the memory back as I walked across the room. *About time.*

I quickly checked myself in the glossy wall, before running the brush through my hair hastily.

I opened the door and my face fell with disappointment. Delaras stood in the doorway. I instantly contemplated shutting the door in her face and locking it. But I didn't know how to lock it; there didn't seem to be locks on any of the doors.

"Good morning, Trixie," Delaras greeted me, her voice slightly husky.

I swallowed. "Delaras."

"May I come in?" Delaras glanced behind me.

"Ah..."

Someone cleared their throat loudly behind her.

Delaras and I both looked around for the source of the sound; my eyes focused on a tall, bulky man with dark skin behind her that I hadn't seen before. He stood with his arms crossed. His brown hair was cut so short that it almost looked shaved.

"Trixie, I'm here to collect you for your training," he growled, his oak-brown eyes glued to Delaras.

I glanced from the stern faced man to Delaras; she looked frustrated. I had a feeling his anger was not aimed at me.

"And who are you?" I asked.

"Name is Jake," he replied. "Kieran was called away today, and he asked me to continue your endurance training."

"Oh," I said.

Disappointment ran through my veins. I had been nervous about seeing him today, but I was also looking forward to seeing those stunning eyes again. I guess that explained why Kieran didn't wake me.

"Delaras, I believe Demetri is looking for you," Jake stated bluntly, turning to Delaras.

Delaras glared at him, her jaw clenched. I watched as she took one last look at me and then stalked down the hallway. Jake watched her round the corner before he spoke again.

"Try to avoid being alone with her if you can." His voice was much softer.

"So you know?" I questioned, raising my eyebrows.

He nodded. "I am one of the council members. We are investigating her."

I looked at the place Delaras had disappeared. Jake followed my gaze.

"Is she a spy for my parents?"

"We think she could be." He sighed. "She doesn't speak much around me. I suspect it's because I can tell if she's lying."

I frowned. I waited for him to continue, watching him expectantly.

"It's my gift." He explained. "Anyone who is nearby, I can feel if they are lying. Not an exciting gift to have, but it's very useful."

"That's incredible. What other special gifts are there?" My mouth hung open.

"Expanding their shields further, repairing broken items, detecting danger," he said. "There are many gifts amongst Soul Weavers."

"Do all Soul Weavers have a special gift?"

"Some." Jake replied, watching me carefully.

Some. But not all.

"Does...Kieran?"

He looked over my face for a moment before he answered. "No."

Nodding, I chewed my lip, mulling over his words.

"Come on, let's go for a run." Jake said as he turned.

"A run?" My eyes shot wide. "Wait...what?"

I THOUGHT WE were heading toward the training room, but Jake led me in the opposite direction.

"So where was Kieran called away to?" I asked.

"He's on a mission with Clara," he replied casually.

I swallowed, my heart skipping a beat. *Clara?*

"With who?"

"Clara, she's his partner."

My jaw dropped. *He had a partner, and he kissed me? Twice!*

Guilt wrapped around me. I had been kissing another girl's man. I closed my mouth before Jake noticed my reaction. *Wait, why was he kissing other girls?* My guilt evaporated as quickly as it had come. I should be angry with *him*. He had played me. *Had he been sucking up to me just so I would forgive him for lying?* Shit. He was just using me.

Arsehole.

Jake stopped, and I almost walked into the back of him. I jumped backwards before he turned to me.

"Okay," Jake mumbled, "let's start here and run around Myrdreya."

"Run around?" I repeated, glancing around us.

We were standing between some buildings on the east side of Myrdreya, opposite the mansion.

I pushed aside the thoughts of Kieran—as best as I could at least.

He nodded. "Yes, you need to run at a pace you are comfortable with while controlling your breathing."

"So I can faint again?" I grumbled sarcastically.

He chuckled. "I heard about that. That's why we are outside—so you have fresh air."

I rolled my eyes.

"Currently, you are at a level five," he stated casually.

My eyebrows pulled together. "What does that mean?"

"Your endurance is nonexistent."

"Great." I said bluntly, raising my eyebrows. "So, what level are you?"

"One," he replied.

"So, one is the best and five is the worst?" Sarcasm played in my voice.

He smirked. "You could say that."

I rolled my eyes again.

"Away you go." He gestured at the path in front of us.

I sighed and jogged. Jake jogged alongside of me; my pace must have been almost a walk for his long legs. I listened to his breathing—it was so even and controlled.

"When you feel comfortable, pick up the pace," he stated.

I wasn't sure if he was being impatient or serious. I allowed myself to jog another 20 metres before I started moving faster. My breathing grew laboured.

Jake kept pace with me, but still breathed evenly—it was as if he was still walking. *How did they do that?* I focused on the sound of his soft breathing and tried to match it.

We ran in unison around Myrdreya for about an hour before Jake finally slowed. I stopped running, my chest rising and falling while I tried to slow my heart rate. I clutched at my side, pushing on the cramping muscle.

"Good job." Jake stated.

A noise that sounded like I was choking escaped my lips. Opening my mouth wide, I sucked in air, trying to ease the pain in my side and the ache in my lungs.

"You have done well today."

"Thanks." I choked out.

"Try to practise on your own again later today," he suggested.

I nodded. "When will Kieran be back?"

Jake looked at me curiously. "Later tonight, I think."

〉〉〉〉● 〈〈〈〈

I HADN'T SEEN Kieran yet, but when I did, I was going to give him my peace of mind.

I had gone for another run around Myrdreya, like Jake had instructed me. I definitely needed a lot of practice.

The cool air was refreshing on my face. After running for half an hour, I slowed to a walk and made my way back through the city. Before I made it to the mansion, Kieran strolled around the corner of the entrance. I paused, my resolve hardening like concrete, but my legs turning to jelly.

"Trixie, what are you doing out here?" He sounded surprised to see me out so late by myself.

Of course, he would be surprised. *He wouldn't want me*

finding him kissing other girls, now would he? Regaining solidity in my legs, I ground my teeth as I stormed up to him.

"You have a *partner*?" I blurted out, louder than necessary.

His eyes widened. "Yes."

"You didn't tell me." My body shook with anger. "And you *kissed* me."

He frowned, his face riddled with confusion. *Seriously? He thought it was normal to be kissing several girls?*

He shook his head. "Wait—you think she's my girlfriend?"

"That's what a partner is...isn't it?" I was standing awkwardly, now confused as well.

He tried to hide a smile, unsuccessfully.

"Why are you smiling?" I demanded angrily, crossing my arms.

"She's not my girlfriend," he announced, the smile on his face grew, his eyebrows raising. "Clara is my mission partner. We partner up to keep each other safe."

Oh. My. God. My cheeks turned tomato red. I felt ridiculous. *How could I be so stupid?* I closed my eyes for a moment, letting out a breath I hadn't realised I was holding.

"I feel flattered," he teased.

Opening my eyes, I saw his smile had grown even wider. He looked so handsome when he smiled.

I rolled my eyes. "Well, I feel *stupid*."

CHANTELLE LAMBERT

Kieran laughed and stepped forward; a deliberate movement that had me rooted in place.

"Don't feel stupid," he replied as he mesmerised me with those dazzling silvery-brown eyes again. "But, just to clarify, you are definitely the only one I'm kissing."

My heart fluttered. He was standing close enough to touch me. I swallowed, totally embarrassed.

"It's late...I better go to bed," I mumbled and slowly turned away, leaving him standing alone.

Walking through the entrance of the mansion, I took the chance to glance back. His gorgeous face was still watching me.

OVER THE FOLLOWING weeks, Kieran continued my endurance training with me outside. To my relief, I didn't faint again. To my surprise, I gradually got better.

"Level Four," Kieran announced at the end of our 20th running session.

I smiled and said playfully, "So, I'm finally moving up in ranks, huh?"

"Finally." He smirked. "But you still have a long way to go."

I sighed. "I know. Thanks for reminding me."

"Now that you are *finally* making progress, we should recheck on your senses."

I cocked my head to the side. "You mean we can

finally go back to the forest?"

"No, I'm afraid not." He shook his head, watching me closely. "They will monitor that forest for your return."

I slowly nodded, my hope vanquished.

"We will go to a mountainside instead."

I smiled. As long as we could leave the city for different scenery, I was pleased. I hadn't been allowed to leave Myrdreya since the encounter with my parents in Elvanor Forest—and I was desperate for some outside adventuring.

Thirteen

BY THE TIME WE RETURNED from our journey to Mount Seaside, I was totally exhausted. My mind and body were worn out from attempting to listen to and recognise my surroundings from a kilometre away.

Kieran was impressed with my senses. He said I was a natural at it, which made me very pleased with myself. However, it also meant I didn't need to venture out of Myrdreya often.

I collapsed on my bed, fully clothed. I closed my eyes.

It was so easy opening my senses compared to opening my heart. Kieran was a nice enough guy. He didn't have a girlfriend like I had wrongly and embarrassingly assumed. He was handsome, strong, kind, and seemed to want to protect me.

I let out my breath slowly. It had almost been a year since Levi had left. A year since I had seen or heard from him after he—I stopped my thoughts there.

He left. *Why am I still holding on?* He's not coming back, and he would freak to know what I have become. He wouldn't understand me and would probably just run away again.

I sat bolt upright. Kieran's face flowed into my mind. I touched my lips with my forefinger; his kiss had tasted so nice. He had held me with more than just force; it had felt like he genuinely cared for me.

I jumped off my bed and headed out into the corridor. Looking around, I could see the corridor was empty. I stared at a flight of stairs; I thought I remembered how to get to his room.

I hurried along the corridor, up the stairs, and then started along the next passage. Yes, I could see his bedroom door ahead. My heart was pounding behind my rib cage. When I reached his door, I paused.

Holding a hand up to knock, I froze. I stared at his frosted glass door. *What if he didn't like me the way I liked him? What if I'd been imagining it this whole time?*

I couldn't move. My limbs had gone to jelly.

My heart was thumping so hard that I could hear it in my ears. *Was I making it all up just to get over Levi?*

I stood frozen outside his door, my hand still poised to knock. The door swung open and caught me off guard.

"Trixie!" Kieran stood in the doorway, surprise on his face.

I dropped my hand quickly and stared at him. He was shirtless. My breath caught. I looked at his chest, then his stomach; he was very muscular. I guess I shouldn't have been surprised.

He cleared his throat. *Oh shoot, he noticed I was looking at his body.* I snapped my eyes back to his face; he was trying to hide a smile.

"Sorry." I didn't know what else to say. I blushed as I diverted my eyes to the floor.

He took a step closer and rested his hand under my chin. He gently pulled my face up to meet his. My heart began pounding faster—I didn't know it was possible to go faster than it already was. His beautiful almond-shaped eyes locked on mine, and I was suddenly swept away.

Without thinking, I threw myself at him. My lips locked onto his as I wrapped my arms around him. I clung to him tightly. His hands were loose around me, like he wasn't sure about kissing me. *Oh, no, had I imagined it all?* I pulled away, breaking our embrace.

Staring up at him, wide-eyed and surprised with myself, I said, "I'm sorry, if you don't want—"

"Why wouldn't I?" He interrupted me and pulled me into his room.

He closed his door, and we stared at each other for a split second before we threw ourselves at each other again. His lips were urgent on mine. His hands were softly searching over my shoulders, my back, and down to my hips. He pressed his body firmly against mine.

His hands continued searching down my body. He gripped my outer thighs under my buttocks and pulled me up onto him. I wrapped my legs around his waist and my arms around his shoulders. We continued to lock lips as he slowly shuffled us over to his bed. He slowly turned us 180 degrees and lowered himself to sit on the bed. I straddled him as I gripped him. His hands were on my back, holding me against his muscular, shirtless body.

Bang, bang, bang.

We pulled apart, and our eyes darted to the door.

"Kieran, are you there?" A voice yelled behind the door.

I scrambled off Kieran and sat on the bed beside him. My heart was going a million miles an hour, and I realised I was out of breath. He kissed me softly on the cheek before standing, making me blush.

I watched as he stood awkwardly by the door, one knee propped forward. *Oh.* I smirked at him and looked away.

He opened the door, only wide enough for him to liaise with whomever stood beyond it.

"Yes?" he said.

"Kieran, oh, you are here," the person said. "Demetri would like to see you."

Kieran sighed. "Is it urgent?"

"I'm afraid so; it involves the girl's parents." I heard the man say.

My smile fell away from my face instantly. I stared at Kieran. His shoulders tensed. My expression was hard. He glanced at me out of the corner of his eye briefly before nodding at the man.

"Okay," he replied. "Tell Demetri I will be there shortly."

He closed the door and walked back over to me. He sat on the bed beside me again and placed a hand on mine. I waited for him to say something.

"We've been watching their movements. Sounds like Demetri has some important information," he explained.

"So that is where you went on your mission today?"

He nodded. "Yes, but we found nothing. Demetri wants to see me for my report from today."

"So, when can I be involved in these meetings? They are my parents, after all."

"Demetri doesn't trust you." Kieran looked away, his voice low.

I swallowed. "Do you? Do you trust me?"

He turned back to me and gazed into my eyes. "Yes, I do."

"You're not..." I began awkwardly, fiddling with my

fingers, "using me for information, right?"

"Of course not." He shook his head with his eyes wide. "You don't think that, do you?"

I looked away for a moment, then shook my head.

"No." I met his eyes again. "I'm just afraid of opening up to someone again."

I couldn't believe I just told him that. I turned away, blushing. His shoulders relaxed, and he leaned toward me. His hand soft on my chin again, he pecked me on the lips.

"I promise," he said, his face still close to mine. "I like you for who you are, not what you know."

My heart skipped a beat. I smiled up at him, slightly embarrassed at asking him that question. *Why was I making a habit of constantly embarrassing myself in front of him?*

"Demetri is waiting for me." He stood, pulling me to my feet and wrapping his arms around my waist. "Will I see you later?"

I nodded.

He leant down, and we locked in another embrace. I was reluctant when he pulled away.

ANOTHER MONTH PASSED by, and Kieran agreed I had improved in my training. We had started my training in magic this morning.

"Focus," he yelled at me for the 10th time.

We hadn't had another intimate moment like the one in his bedroom. He had been too focused on my training — much to my disappointment. Or he was off on missions with Jake or Clara. Where they went all the time, I didn't know. I was being kept in the dark. I wondered if he regretted kissing me and was avoiding talking to me about it.

"I'm trying!" I almost yelled back at him, crossing my arms.

He stepped forward, taking my hands in his.

"Sorry." He breathed. "You can do it. I know you can."

I looked up into his eyes; mesmerising as usual. He kissed me softly on my lips and then leant his forehead on mine. Maybe I was wrong; he just had a lot going on.

"Close your eyes and imagine the magic inside you," he suggested.

I closed my eyes, letting out a slow breath.

He stepped back as he released my hands from his.

"Think about what it looks like, feels like," he continued in a whisper. "What colour is it? Is it blue? Is it green?"

I scrunched up my eyes as I thought about the magic I apparently had inside me. *Was magic coloured?* Oh, of course it was. Kieran's was purple. I began wondering what colour mine would be and what it would look like.

What colour was it the day my life did a back-flip? The day my life had truly fallen apart and turned into a whirlwind. The day that man, with pure evil in his eyes, had murdered Kiarra. The day I had somehow slowed down time. My fingers began to tingle as I revisited the heart-breaking memory.

"Good start," Kieran softly said.

I opened my eyes, blinking, slightly dazed.

"Your magic is turquoise," he announced in reply to my confusion.

"How do you know that?" I asked.

A smirk played at the corner of his mouth. "Electric energy appeared at your fingertips, and it was turquoise."

My jaw dropped.

"But how did I—?"

"What were you thinking?"

"I was thinking about your magic being purple and then about how I..." I trailed off.

"How you what?" he questioned.

I hesitated, shifting from one foot to the other.

"How I slowed down time before you showed up."

He stared at me in disbelief. "You what?"

I instantly wondered if I shouldn't have told him that. *Did it make me a freak?*

"I-I slowed down time." I stumbled over my words. "It was like I had frozen the Soul Hunter in place."

"That is extraordinary," Kieran stated. "Some Soul Weavers have an additional power, but I have never heard of yours before."

"Is that a good or bad thing?" I asked warily.

"It's neither; it's just extraordinary for us to have another gifted Soul Weaver on our side." He beamed. "What did you do? Or what did he do? To bring on the stasis?"

"Stasis," I repeated, thinking back to that horrifying day. My heart tried to leap from my chest as I recounted the details of my best friend's death.

"H-he snapped Kiarra's neck, and I screamed." My eyes became teary; I blinked as I continued. "Next thing I knew, he wasn't moving and a ball of electricity hit him in slow motion."

"A form of stasis..." he said, more to himself than to me. Then he queried, "Was that ball turquoise?"

I thought about it for a moment. "Yes, it was."

Kieran nodded in understanding.

"There's only a few of us who have gifts. You are lucky to be one of them," he announced proudly, grinning from ear to ear.

I stared at him with my mouth ajar. My world really was changing—from learning that I had magic in my veins to discovering that I could also slow down time. Nothing was as it seemed.

"You know, if you keep your mouth open long enough, you might catch flies this time."

I thought about his statement for a moment. "But the shield keeps insects out."

Kieran laughed. I laughed with him.

"Well, at least I know you can accidentally summon

your magic when you're in danger," he said.

We laughed again. It was music to my ears.

>>>⟨◉⟩<<<

KIERAN ENSURED I trained every day with my magic. Every day, I improved. Every week, I learnt a new spell. He taught me how to move objects around the room, and how to lock and unlock my bedroom door using magic. He explained these spells were simple and required little concentration. Of course, he was right.

"Now that you have that mastered," he said after two hours of learning the shielding spell. "Let's see how you go with a blast spell."

"I'm not attacking you," I retorted immediately.

His mouth curled into a smirk. "I'm used to being beaten up."

I frowned. "Domestic violence is not okay."

"Not beaten up in that way," he replied. "You're very literal, aren't you? I have trained many Soul Weavers; I act as their training dummy. Now, it's my turn to act as yours."

I shook my head. "But I could hurt you."

"Don't worry. You won't hurt me." He stepped toward me, close enough that I could smell his deodorant; it was a musky pine-wood smell.

I looked at his face warily.

"Trust me," he said, placing a hand softly on my cheek.

Leaning into his cupped hand, I relaxed and nodded. "Okay. So, what do I do?"

He took a few steps backwards. I watched as he retreated a couple of metres away.

"Focus on your magic. Pretend I am attacking you, and you are defending yourself," he explained. "Say Ruproco when you are ready."

"Rupruso?"

"Ru-pro-co." He sounded out.

"Right. Ruproco."

I squared my shoulders and planted my feet firmly on the ground. Observing his face, I took a slow breath in and out.

"Ruproco," I said, with my hand outstretched.

A small, pale ball of energy flew toward him and quickly dissipated. He stepped back slightly as if a wind had blown at him, causing him to lose his footing.

"Good try. I felt the force, but not strong enough," he said, stepping forward a few steps. "Try again."

I took another breath and repeated, "Ruproco."

My spell was more substantial this time and less faint in colour. He fell backwards onto the ground. It appeared he had been pushed in the stomach and had been winded.

"Are you okay?" I quickly asked.

He raised his hand, waving at me as he stood back up. "All good. That was better, but you aren't trying hard enough to hurt me."

"That's because I don't want to hurt you," I argued.

"Trixie, you can't learn if you don't push yourself," he said simply.

I glanced over at another pair of Soul Weavers practising their magic. A woman beckoned her opponent. He threw a spell at her; his magic was pale green. She spun to the right, out of the path of the ball. He immediately threw another spell at her, and she dodged it again.

"Why aren't you trying to dodge my spell?" I asked curiously, turning back to Kieran.

"They are practising dodging. You are practising hitting the target and blasting him into the air."

"Into the air?" I raised my eyebrows. "Now I'm definitely not going to attack you."

He laughed. "Come on, Trixie, show me what you got. Or I will have to attack you and see you fly."

I blinked, staring at his expression. I didn't know whether to take him seriously.

"Come on, 30 seconds, or I will throw a spell at you. Thirty...29...28..."

"You're not serious." I choked out a nervous laugh, shifting awkwardly.

"I'm dead serious. Twenty-four...," he continued counting.

I swallowed and stared at his lips as he counted backwards. He *was* being serious. My heart started pounding. I didn't want to hurt him, but I didn't want to get hurt either.

"Eighteen...17...you're running out of time." Kieran's expression was determined.

I glanced at the other pair in the training room. They were still dodging each other's spells.

"Twelve...11..."

He was still counting, and he had his hand outstretched toward me. The thumping in my rib cage grew stronger as I became more anxious.

"Eight...seven...make your choice, Trix."

Swallowing down bile, I looked into his eyes. *Surely he wouldn't attack me, would he?*

"Three...two..."

Swirls of purple appeared at his fingertips. My eyes widened.

I threw my hand up and yelled, "RUPROCO!"

An almost blinding ball of turquoise electric energy erupted from my fingers. It closed the distance between him and me within moments, and it left me staring in shock. Kieran was thrown off his feet, into the air, and landed five metres from where he had been standing.

"KIERAN!" I shouted as I ran across the room.

He pushed himself up and looked up at me as I approached.

I stopped a metre from him; he was grinning.

"You just needed some persuasion." He laughed.

I heard laughter from the other pair in the room; I glanced over my shoulder and saw them watching us. Blushing, I turned away from them and stared at Kieran.

"It's not funny. I was freaking out."

"I wouldn't have hurt you. But you wouldn't have thrown such a powerful spell at me either," he said as he stood up.

"Did I hurt you?" I questioned, looking over his bodice, arms, and legs.

He shook his head. "No, of course not. I had a damage reduction spell on me."

"A what?"

"A spell to reduce the amount of pain inflicted. It felt like a tickle." He laughed again. "Well, and a whoosh of wind from being thrown through the air."

Slightly annoyed he didn't tell me about his damage reduction, I was suddenly aware I was holding a breath. I exhaled with a sigh. He took a step forward and took my hands. I was conscious of the others in the room watching us, but he didn't seem to care.

"If you let yourself, you will be a natural at magic," Kieran said softly, his gaze holding me mesmerised.

KIERAN PUSHED MY physical and magic training every day. We had a daily routine; wake up, run around the city for an hour, relax and practise my senses in the garden, and then go to the training room to learn magic.

I could feel myself growing stronger. I could run around Myrdreya longer before I got exhausted. And I wasn't fainting anymore. My senses were very strong; I could hear chattering from the other side of the city. I was always careful not to listen in on private conversations — no matter how tempting they were. Kieran said it was forbidden and I wouldn't like the consequences.

Once an ordinary girl, I was now thriving with magic I had never known I possessed until a short time ago. I felt like I had finally found my place in this world, who I really was, and where I truly belonged.

Fourteen

TRIXIE

"TIME FOR PORTAL TRAINING," Kieran announced as I opened my bedroom door at eight in the morning.

It was the end of summer, my favourite season; however, being inside the force field of the island, we couldn't feel any difference.

"I finally get to learn to summon portals?" I gasped with excitement.

I was already fully dressed, complete with my black and white sneakers; I had donned a pair of black leggings and a purple tank top. My unnaturally straight platinum blonde hair hung around my shoulders.

He grinned. "You sure do!"

I threw my fist in the air like an excited child. Kieran laughed at my childishness but then smiled at me with heart-warming eyes. He really seemed to like me for who I was.

"Come on, let's head to the gardens to practise there." He stepped aside for me to exit my room.

We left the mansion and crossed Myrdreya to the gardens. Someone was standing in the gardens when we arrived.

"Tayla." Kieran greeted the woman.

"Hi, Kieran," Tayla said, "and this must be Trixie."

I smiled at her. She was dressed casually in white three-quarter leggings and a lime-green loose v-neck top.

"How are you finding your training so far?" Tayla asked, her amber eyes glowing in the sunlight.

"It's definitely interesting," I replied, looking at how her pixie cut black hair complimented her amber eyes.

Tayla smirked. "Well, it's about to get even more interesting."

I glanced at Kieran, and he shrugged at me.

"Well, let's begin," she announced. "Portal from here across the garden. Think about the place you want to portal to."

Oh, because it was that easy. *Was she not going to give me more guidance?*

I looked around the garden; there was a nice open area by some bushes only five metres away. I was suddenly very nervous. If I aimed to land in the middle of the clear area, then I should be safe...*right?*

"Close your eyes and think about what you are about to do. Imagine the portal in front of you, the swirling motion of it," Tayla instructed me. "Now put your hand out in front of you and feel the magic at your fingertips. When you are ready, say the word Rumodo."

I frowned.

"You never said anything when you made portals?" I asked Kieran.

"With practise you won't need to either." He said, smiling.

Taking a breath, I closed my eyes. I felt the energy of my magic form at my fingertips almost immediately. I pushed against it, forcing my magic from my hand.

"Rumodo," I breathed.

A quick whoosh of air sounded to my right—Kieran.

Opening my eyes slowly, I found a swirling turquoise portal in front of me. My lips parted. In the middle of it, I could faintly see the garden.

"Go ahead." Tayla said, nodding toward it.

Hesitantly, I stepped through the portal. I barely felt the gravity lift from under my feet before I touched back down again. I stood in front of the bush—exactly where I had wanted to land.

My portal disappeared as I turned around to look back

at it. Kieran and Tayla were staring at me. Kieran was grinning. I was slightly dumbfounded that I had just successfully made a portal.

"Well done," Tayla said. "Now let's try further. Walk up that path and then portal back to us. This time, try to do it faster."

I walked up the path she indicated. I didn't know how far I was meant to go, so I just kept walking.

"That's far enough!" Kieran yelled out to me.

I turned around and saw Tayla glaring at Kieran as she said something to him. I was too far away to hear, and their conversation stopped before I could open my senses to listen. Tayla nodded at me.

Once again, I closed my eyes, imagining the garden. I placed my hand out in front and felt the now familiar magic soaring through my veins.

"Rumodo."

I opened my eyes just as the swirling energy erupted from my fingers again, forming a portal. Smiling, I stepped through and landed in the same place in the garden as I did before.

Turning around to face them again, I grinned, feeling incredibly proud of myself. Tayla was nodding in approval.

"You're a natural. Let's take it one step further," she said. "I'm pleased with how easily you did that."

Kieran glanced sideways at the woman, narrowing his eyes. My stomach lurched. I suddenly felt nervous again at his reaction to her words.

"I will portal you somewhere, and you need to portal yourself back here. As long as you focus on your task, you will be fine."

My heart skipped a beat, but I squared my shoulders and nodded. She opened a pure white portal—to what looked like a dark room. I didn't think anyone would have white magic since it's not actually a colour.

I took another breath and stepped through.

I landed in complete darkness. It was eerie and smelt like dirt. Reaching my hands out in front of my body, I felt around the room. Nothing except for four walls; I couldn't even feel a door. Hearing my heartbeat thumping in my ears, I was very anxious.

My hands searched the walls again; I was trapped. No door. Panic set in. *What if I couldn't get back out of here? I would starve in the darkness, alone.* A shiver ran down my back, but it wasn't even cold.

"Focus," I said out loud to myself, remembering my task.

Standing still in the dark room, I imagined the garden again. I imagined Kieran's handsome face as he waited for me to reappear. Closing my eyes and keeping my focus, my magic erupted again.

"Rumodo," I whispered in the lonely room.

I snapped my eyes open to see a turquoise portal waiting for me. And I immediately recognised the garden beyond. I smiled and stepped through.

I was relieved to find myself standing back in front of Kieran and Tayla. Kieran's features relaxed when I glanced at him with the reassurance I was okay.

"Good, well done. A bit slow that time, but I'm pleased you still managed to do it. Again," she said, summoning up another portal.

This portal was very bright—so bright there was no destination discernible in it. I peered into the swirling vortex, unsure of where it might take me.

"Tayla..." Kieran said warningly.

"Step through," she instructed, ignoring Kieran.

Glancing from Kieran to Tayla, I took a deep breath and stepped into the portal.

I instantly began falling. But this time, the sensation wasn't stopping; I was actually falling. I screamed and started waving my arms around, which was ridiculous, considering it would not help me.

Shaking my head, I looked around. Patches of cloud surrounded me. I looked up and saw the glass island growing further and further away.

My heart pounded in my ears, along with the wind; it was deafening. *Did something go wrong? Had she dropped me off the island on purpose?* Panic filled my body as I free-fell from the island; the floating glass growing further away.

The falling slowed. I could see the texture of the clouds I passed through. I had slowed down time again. A mix of relief and panic overflowed me.

No one was here to save me. Kieran couldn't get to me. I had to save myself.

As I continued to fall slowly through the air, I closed my eyes and tried to focus on the incantation I had been taught.

Opening my eyes, I focused below me. I started calling out the word with my hand outstretched.

"Rumodo."

Nothing happened.

"Rumodo!" I yelled louder.

Still nothing. My eyes watered; I wasn't sure if it was from the wind or if I was crying. I rapidly shook my head, squeezing my eyes shut tight.

Snapping my eyes open again, I focused below and screamed, "RUMODO!"

Turquoise iridescent swirls erupted from my fingertips, quickly forming an oval shape below me. I plummeted straight into it.

I hit the ground hard. Grasping my head in my hands, I rolled over to my side. I could see I was lying on the glass ground. *Looks like I'm back in Myrdreya.*

"Trix?" a familiar voice asked; a hand touched my shoulder softly.

I adverted my focus from the smoothness of the glass ground and looked straight up into Kieran's eyes. I said nothing. His fingers swept across my cheek—wiping away my tears. I reached up and wrapped my arms tightly around him. His arms clasped around me.

"Trixie, are you okay?" he asked, straining under my pressure.

I held onto him and replied in a raspy voice, "I'm okay."

His body tensed.

"Are you insane?" Kieran suddenly yelled.

"She was safe," Tayla announced, waving him away. "She had you."

"You threw her off the city!" Kieran bellowed. "She wasn't ready for that!"

"She got back here, didn't she?"

Kieran's jawed clenched against my cheek. His anger rolling off him. He pulled me to my feet but didn't let me go. I leant against him, thankful for his body to support mine. I vaguely glanced around and recognised the garden. Relief washed over me, but I continued to cling to Kieran. I had done it.

"Come on. Enough for today," Kieran muttered as he led us away from the garden.

⤐⤐⤐◉⤏⤏⤏

LEANING ON MY balcony railing, I stared up at the twinkling balls of fire. Myrdreya was so high in the sky that I could clearly see millions of stars. Ever so slowly, the stars moved as they rotated around Earth.

Earth. *Were we even still on Earth? Where were we?* I still had so many unanswered questions.

Levi and I used to lie on a blanket in the middle of a field watching the stars for hours. We would get eaten by mosquitoes, but we didn't care. I smiled at the thought of how itchy we were later; we would scratch each other out of our miseries.

My smile faded as the memory turned to pain. My heart started beating so hard against my chest that I couldn't breathe. I opened my mouth, gasping for fresh air. The world was crashing down on me.

The balcony railing buckled under my hands. Twisting and opening a gap wide enough for a person. It was almost inviting to just jump off right now and make it all be over.

Closing my eyes, I forced the memory from my mind. *Stop torturing yourself like this.* I shook my head as if I could shake the thought of Levi out of it. Taking deep breaths, my heart slowed. I opened my eyes. The railing was back to its usual architecture. Sighing, I stared at the moon.

This was all too much. Tears rolled down my cheeks.

My legs suddenly moved as though some kind of force was pulling them along. I left my room and made my way to the portal room. No one was there. I thought about the forest near my parents' old house; I used to hide in it when I was angry or upset as a child.

Holding my hand out in front of me, I had the urge to go there. I thought hard about the forest, how the trees looked and smelt.

"Rumodo," I said.

Swirls formed, rotating in front of my fingers until they grew, and a portal floated in front of me. I smiled, proud of myself.

Fifteen

KIERAN

A SHIVER DOWN MY SPINE awoke me from my slumber. Rolling over, I threw the sheet off and walked over to the balcony. Catching sight of someone going for a night stroll, I paused.

Trixie.

I stepped out onto the balcony and watched her for a moment. She was walking through the city with no shoes on. *That's strange.* My eyebrows pulled together. *Does she sleep walk?*

I pulled on some shoes and a jacket and hurried out of

my bedroom door and down the corridor. *What is she doing out at this time of night – and with no shoes on?*

Observing that no one else was following, I headed through the buildings in the direction I had seen her walking. I looked around every corner in search of her, but she was nowhere to be seen.

My pulse thrummed in my ears.

I ducked behind a tree and cleared my mind. Closing my eyes, I focused on her face and listened. Through the city, my senses took me. I glimpsed her wavy hair rounding a corner, and I snapped my eyes open.

"The portal room?" I whispered to myself as I started running.

As I reached the portal room, I slowed to a walk. I crept up to the doorway and peered in. Trixie stepped through a portal and vanished. I threw my hand out as her portal swirled and faded.

I sprinted forward and dove into her disappearing portal.

The forest I landed in was gloomy. Trixie was nowhere in sight. I recognised it instantly, though. I had been here before.

Sixteen

LACKING OXYGEN, I RAN FOR my life.

If they caught me, I was as good as dead.

A shiver ran down my spine. One of them was getting close on my heels. I refused to look back, forcing myself to focus on forward movement. Winding my way through the forest, I leapt over small boulders and broken branches. Twigs and more dead leaves crushed under my feet—and moments later, under the feet of my closest pursuer.

Thump. Thump.

My heart hammered as I ducked under another low-hanging branch. Catching my foot on yet another tree root, I stumbled. The ground came closer to my face as I fell to the earth, collapsing onto my hands and knees. I whimpered as my palm came into contact with a sharp rock, slicing it open—instantly reminded of the wound on my face. They both stung.

My pursuer was upon me, grabbing my shoulders and rolling me over. He pinned me to the forest floor. Damp dirt mushed into my hair, and a sharp stick dug into my back. I wriggled under his weight as he straddled me, holding my wrists down. My unsteady breath escaped my lips as I thrashed beneath him.

"Let...me..."

"Trix?" The sound of his voice startled me.

Hearing my nickname, I stopped struggling against him and stared up at his face. My mouth dropped open as my breath caught in my throat. My eyes widened as I stared at the familiar face. His dark skin, cheekbones, jawline, and ice-blue eyes were how I remembered them. I couldn't believe who was staring back down at me.

My eyes were wide, staring, feeling hurt all over again.

"*Levi?*"

"Get out of here," he stated, pulling me to my feet.

Confusion washed over me, my heart aching. "Excuse me?"

"Go, now."

"But—you disappeared." *Was he in front of me at all?*

"I'm sorry. It was to keep you safe." His face contorted for a split second before he said bluntly, "Now, run!"

He shoved me backward, away from him. I planted my bare feet down, steadying myself.

"I don't understand; you're one of *them*?" I swallowed. "You're a Soul Hunter?"

He nodded, averting his eyes from me. "Trixie, run, before they capture you."

My eyes darted behind him into the dark trees. There was no one else in sight, but I could hear the rustling of the bushes and the crunching of branches.

"We know you're out here! We will find you," a husky voice yelled.

"Now! *Go!*" Levi pleaded.

I looked at him for a moment before turning on my bare feet. Running as fast as I could, I jumped and swerved around the trees.

"She went that way." I heard him say in the distance.

No way. He ratted me out. Why would he do that? I pushed myself forward, running faster than I had ever done before with bare feet. I ducked under a tree branch and leaped over a small moss-covered boulder. Slipping into a mud puddle, I grabbed the nearest trunk. *Shit!* The cut on my hand stung against the bark. I groaned as I attempted to dust the dirt out of the wound.

The voices and running footsteps were growing further and further away. Sighing with relief, I leant against a tree. I allowed myself to slide down the trunk and sit on the damp earth. My heart threatened to leap out of my chest and my lungs were on the verge of collapse. My feet were sore from running on dirt and sticks. Mud caked between my toes. *Argh, gross.*

I placed my head in my hands and leant on my knees. Tears welled up in my eyes. I never thought I would see Levi again, let alone see him as a Soul Hunter chasing me.

So, in the past 6 months, my best friend had been murdered, I found out my parents were Dark Soul Weavers, and now my ex-boyfriend was a Soul Hunter who apparently left for my safety. *What else?*

My head was a whirlwind. It was spinning, and I didn't know if I could stand up and make it back to Myrdreya. Tears ran down my cheeks as I hugged myself in the dark, damp forest. My muscles vibrated. *Or was I shaking?* I wasn't sure.

"Trixie!"

I lifted my head, dazed. "Kieran?"

"I have been looking for you everywhere…" His words caught in his throat as he saw the tears running down my face. "Are you okay? Are you hurt?"

He crouched down in front of me, inspecting me.

I shook my head. "No, I'm okay." Well, maybe mentally hurt, but I didn't want to say that out loud.

He pulled something out of my hair and let it fall to the ground. A twig. *Oh god, I must look like a mess.*

He cupped my cheek. "You've got a cut on your cheek."

"Tree branch." I choked.

His eyebrows pulled together as he studied my face.

"Don't worry, it doesn't hurt anymore." I wiped away the tears.

He grabbed my wrist. Gently, he turned my palm upward to expose the wound.

"And a cut on your hand." He said. "Any others?"

I shook my head, staring at my dirty feet.

"Well, my feet."

He sighed. "Why are you out here by yourself? The Soul Hunters could have found you."

"They did," I mumbled.

"What?" he questioned, his eyes wide.

"They found me. I ran and..." *Should I tell him of my encounter with my ex-boyfriend?* "And got away."

His eyes narrowed. "They are fast. How did you get away so easily?"

Watching his face, I sighed. Of course, he saw straight through me. He raised his eyebrows, waiting.

"I-I ran into my ex-boyfriend." I laughed awkwardly. "Turns out he's a Soul Hunter."

Kieran let out a breath and sat on the damp ground in front of me. I eyed him warily for a moment before looking away, biting my lip.

"Are you okay?" He asked as he shifted on the dirt.

I nodded. "Yeah."

"Is that why you broke up?"

"I guess you could say that." I fiddled with a fallen wet

leaf, crushing it between my fingertips.

"I'm sorry."

"He ran off and vanished. I didn't know why. For months and months, I was miserable. My best friend," I paused. This was the first time in a while I had spoken about either of them. "Kiarra noticed the mark on my neck the day you rescued me. I guess he had seen the mark and knew what I was, so he left."

Kieran nodded. He stayed silent. We both looked at the ground while I continued to fiddle with the leaf. I had never intended to tell Kieran about Levi—let alone tell him I had moped around for months because of it. But, as they say, *the cat was out of the bag* now.

"I can't believe he's one of them," I mumbled.

Seventeen

TRIXIE

BEFORE THE SUN ROSE, I tossed under the covers, unable to keep my eyes closed. Kiarra's horrified face swam under my eyelids every time I closed them. Dreaming about her death haunted me. Her lifeless body, her staring eyes.

I had left her body in my house. Surely someone had found her body by now, and my name was plastered all over the world for murder.

But I didn't murder my best friend. I watched her die at the hands of my true enemy—Soul Hunters. My heart skipped a beat. Levi was a Soul Hunter. He knew months before I did who I was.

I climbed out of bed and slipped into clean clothes. Crossing the room, I put my shoes on and opened my door. I popped my head out into the hallway to see if anyone was around. It was empty. I closed the door quietly behind me and hurried down the corridor.

Upon reaching the portal room, I practised what Tayla had taught me. I closed my eyes, cleared my mind, and put my right hand out in front of me. I thought about where I wanted to go. The magic grew within me and I opened my eyes to see the swirling turquoise magic erupting from my fingertips. A portal formed in front of me. My lips parted. I hadn't spoken, and the portal worked.

I recognised the trees in the swirling portal as the forest near my house. Without hesitation, I stepped through.

The gravity was ripped out from under me as I floated through the portal for a moment. My feet touched solid ground, and the portal vanished behind me. There was a very light breeze through the trees. It was dark here, but dawn was approaching, so I needed to be quick.

I raced through the trees, into my street, and found my house quickly. There was an eerie darkness about the house that used to be my home. The gardens were overgrown, and the windows were thick with scum. No one was living here.

I paused on the threshold, taking a breath to calm my growing nerves.

I tried the doorknob, and it clicked open. *Not even locked? Had no one been here at all?* Entering the lounge room, I stopped and stared. The place had been ransacked. I sighed. That explained why I could get into the house so easily. Kiarra's lifeless body was also gone; there was no sign of it ever being here.

I looked up at the photo frames on the wall. Relief washed over me. The photo of Kiarra and me was still there, intact. It was the last photo taken of us together; Kiarra had gotten it printed and framed for me. I reached up and carefully lifted it off its hook to take back to Myrdreya with me.

"I thought I might find you here."

Startled, I spun around and held my hand out, ready to defend myself.

"Levi?" I was stunned.

He smiled weakly at me.

I dropped my hand. "What are you doing here?"

"I had to see you again."

"How did you know I would come back here?" I eyed him curiously.

"It's your home." He shrugged, pointing to the frame in my hand. "I figured you would eventually come back to collect anything of importance."

Staying silent, I stared at him. He stepped closer. He was standing right before me; his breath on my face was like a light warm breeze.

"I've missed you," he said in that sweet tone I had fallen in love with.

"I…"

He pressed his mouth against mine. Not just any kiss—it was a kiss of pure passion and love. I allowed myself to be wrapped in his arms, melting into his touch. The photograph was still in my hands, held loose at my side. My mind was taken over by the passion he possessed. It was the kiss I remembered before he left.

What am I doing? I broke away abruptly. Stepping back, panting, I gently pushed him to arm's length. He stared at me, his eyes grazing over my stunned expression. A crease formed on his forehead.

"I'm sorry." I shook my head. "I can't."

"Trix, I love you."

I swallowed, closing my eyes for a moment. *How do I deal with this right now?* He abandoned me—just like my parents did.

"I have always loved you. I'm so sorry for leaving." He said, his voice pleading.

Words evaded me. *How did he expect that I still trusted or loved him?* A part of my heart was still entwined with his, but I wasn't telling him that. His ice-blue eyes bore into mine.

"I have to get back," I mumbled.

"Please," he reached for me. "Give me another chance—."

"A Soul Hunter killed Kiarra," I stated, cutting him off as I observed his face.

His eyes widened. "What?"

I stared at him.

"Wait…you don't think I did it?" He asked.

"No."

He put his hands up in front of his body. "I had nothing to do it with it! I didn't even know…I'm sorry."

I gritted my teeth. I didn't want his pity.

"They aren't supposed to kill innocents…" he said.

"Innocents?" I repeated, my voice turning cold. "So what does that make me? Am I not innocent?"

"You…uh…"

I raised my eyebrows and crossed my arms. "So, because I'm a Soul Weaver, I'm not innocent? At least we don't go around killing people."

"That's why I left. So they wouldn't find you…to protect you."

"You didn't protect me," I whispered. "They found me and took my best friend away."

The door burst open. Levi and I snapped our eyes to the doorway.

"DUCK, TRIXIE!"

Kieran stood with his hand outstretched. Before I could stop him, he let a fireball fly. I threw myself to the ground, shielding the photo frame beneath me. Crouched on the floor, I turned my head to see Levi smash into the opposite wall and collapse to the ground. Gasping, I scrambled to stand. Kieran held his hand out again, ready to throw another orb.

I jumped between him and Levi with my hands out in front of me. "WAIT!"

Kieran stared at me, his eyes ablaze. "What are you doing? He's a Soul Hunter."

"I know," I said and glanced back at Levi, "and my ex-boyfriend."

I saw a flash of pain cross Levi's face at my words. Kieran looked Levi up and down as if accessing him.

"Let's go. Now." Kieran said.

I nodded and stepped forward. I paused when Levi's pleading voice reached my ears.

"Trix, please…"

Looking back at Levi, I gave him a disappointing glare before walking out the door. Kieran followed me down the street without a word.

⫸⫸⫸◉⫷⫷⫷

"WHAT WERE YOU thinking, going back there?" Kieran blurted out when we arrived back in the portal room. "You just took off again!"

"It was my home." I muttered.

I swallowed. He had never been angry at me before. My forehead creased as I frowned.

"How do I protect you if you keep doing this?"

"I never asked for your protection." I bellowed back,

gritting my teeth. "I never asked for any of this!"

Kieran's face was unreadable as he stared at me. I closed my eyes for a moment and inhaled.

"I had to see if Kiarra was still there," I whispered, reopening my eyes.

His skin softened as he stepped toward me. I hesitated. He pulled me into an embrace; the memory of Levi leaped into my mind and I instantly felt guilty. I wondered if I should tell Kieran or if I should just forget it ever happened.

"Her body was moved soon after I brought you to Myrdreya." He looked down at me.

"Why didn't you tell me sooner?" I asked bluntly.

"I-I don't know." Kieran said. "I'm sorry, I should have told you."

"Yes, you should have. Where did she get moved to? Everyone must think it was me?" I panicked, pinching the bridge of my nose.

Kieran shook his head. "No one thinks it was you. We made sure that Soul Hunter got the blame for her death. He was convicted of her murder a few days ago."

I sighed in relief, dropping my hand away from my face. It relieved me that my face wasn't plastered everywhere for murder. And I was relieved the actual killer had been caught.

"Thank you," I said.

"You can thank Demetri," he replied with a small smile.

I nodded. "I will—next time I see him."

"Shall we get back before anyone knows you snuck out?" He smirked.

I smiled. "Sounds like a good idea."

We left the portal room. To my relief, no one was in sight.

Kieran entwined his hand in mine.

"Hold on, how did you know I snuck out?" I asked, looking at him.

"I…" He seemed to search for words.

I raised my eyebrows.

"I decided to go for a morning walk, but saw you hurrying into the portal room again." Kieran answered sheepishly.

"Oh. That would explain why you got to my house so fast, too."

He nodded.

The sun had finally burst over the city as we entered the mansion. We walked hand in hand up to the bedroom quarters. We reached my corridor and stopped at the bottom of the stairs, which led to his room.

"Did you—erm—did you want to come back to my room?" he asked.

I looked at him. A lump formed in my throat, and butterflies flew around my stomach. His stunning silvery-brown eyes stared back at me, and his lips were slightly parted.

"We both need sleep," he said. "But I thought you

might like to come with me."

I considered his words for a moment before nodding. My heart started pounding again; it did that a lot when I was around him — *why wouldn't it?*

We turned up the flight of stairs and strolled down the familiar corridor to his room. We entered his bedroom, and he closed the door behind us.

"We have the morning off, so we can have a sleep in," he said, taking off his shoes.

I followed suit and slipped my shoes off as well.

"Sounds great. I didn't sleep well last night," I said in a soft voice.

I turned around and saw him pulling his shirt off over his head and throwing it into the laundry basket. I swallowed. He walked over to the curtains and closed them to block out the sunlight.

"That sun can be awfully bright at this time."

I nodded. "Mmhmm, yes, it can be."

There was still enough light in the room that I could see his outline as he walked over to me. My eyes adjusted, and his face became clearly visible through the dim lighting. I forgot I was still holding the photo frame — until Kieran carefully pried it from my hand and placed it on the bookshelf behind me.

"That's Kiarra?" he asked softly, looking at the photo.

I glanced at Kiarra's smiling face and nodded. He entwined his hand in mine again. His other hand found my hip. He pulled me in closer, my body now right against his. My heart began thumping faster.

I placed my free hand on his naked chest; his skin was soft and smooth. Releasing my other hand, he put his hand on my other hip. He leaned down toward me and planted his lips against mine. His kiss was soft but passionate — just the way I liked it.

He gripped my hips harder as he held me against his body. The hand on my right hip relaxed and started moving up toward my lower back. He found his way under my shirt and glided smoothly over my skin. His kiss became more urgent, and I felt his tongue playing with my mine.

My free hand wrapped around his neck as I returned his embrace. While slowly stepping backwards, one foot at a time, he pulled me with him. When we reached the bed, he let himself collapse on it, but he released me as he did so. I stood in front of him for a moment, looking down at him. Reaching for the hem of my shirt, I pulled it off over my head and dropped it on the ground next to me.

Kieran reached out and put his hands on my hips again, leaning forward. He began kissing my stomach; he started at the rim of my jeans and slowly worked his way up toward my bra. I closed my eyes. He stood up and kissed in between my breasts and then continued up my chest to my neck.

I let out a small moan and allowed him to take control over me. I wrapped my arms around his muscular body.

He kissed along my jawbone and then found his way to my lips again.

He pulled away suddenly. My heart dropped, and I snapped my eyes open. He stood nearby, leaning over the bed. A whoosh of air escaped my lips. He threw back the covers of the bedding and then came straight back to me. I allowed him to pull me into his bed. Jeans were very awkward in bed; so thick and stiff.

He laid beside me, holding my body against his. His right hand softly flowed down my skin; he found my hip again. He then slowly made his way toward the front of my jeans—he seemed to be giving me time to object. I didn't.

He gripped the button and unbuttoned it within seconds. I held my breath as he was then unzipping. His hand went back to my hip, pulling me forward.

Inhaling deeply through my nose, his lips found mine again, and I wandered my hand toward his pants. His pants were a lighter cloth fabric for easy movement. I noticed there was no button earlier, so I just pulled at the side of them to show that I wanted them off.

He got the hint and pulled his pants off, leaving just cloth boxers on. When he came back to me, he leant down to kiss my stomach again. His hands gripped onto the top of my jeans and began pulling them down. I wriggled to help him pull them off and then my pants joined his on the ground.

He laid back down next to me, and I wrapped my leg

around his waist. He kissed my neck again as he wrapped his arms around me. I could feel him lightly thrusting against me, and my heart pounded heavily in my chest. I didn't want him to stop; I wanted more. Gripped his shoulders, I pulled him on top of me.

This was the first time I had heard laboured breathing from him. He breathed heavily in my ears, giving me goosebumps down my spine. I held him against me and returned his passionate desire.

Eighteen

TRIXIE

SOMETHING MOVED BESIDE ME. I opened my eyes. It had grown much lighter in the room. Kieran was lying soundlessly in bed with a sheet over his body. I sat up and realised I was still naked from hours before.

I smiled to myself as I glanced over at Kieran. The sheet covered his buttocks, but it revealed his smooth back.

Swinging my legs out of his bed, I picked up my clothes and put them back on. I stood up and looked through the see-through roof and saw the sun high in the sky — must be midday.

"Sneaking off?"

I flinched, looking over at him, and said, "no, of course not."

"Did you sleep well?" Kieran said.

He rolled over, exposing the tight muscles in his stomach; my breath caught in my throat as I stared at how gorgeous he was.

I nodded. "And you?"

He pushed himself up. "Yes. I definitely needed that extra sleep."

My mouth curved into a smile. He climbed out of bed and stood up, facing away. My lips parted; I couldn't look away. My eyes grazed over his shoulders, his back muscles, and his gorgeous muscular buttocks. I swallowed and walked over to him.

He glanced over his shoulder at me. I placed a hand on his shoulder and stood directly in front of him. He looked deeply into my eyes; it was like he was trying to see what I was thinking.

I reached up to kiss him, and he bent down to meet me. His arms locked around my body, and I wrapped mine around his shoulders. Our embrace was soft and passionate. My mind let go, letting any thoughts get whisked away. He made me feel so calm, like my world was finally coming together again.

There was a sudden bang in the distance. We broke

apart, but our hands remained entwined.

"What was that?" We both chimed together.

He picked up his boxers, putting them on as he hurried over and pulled the curtains open. Sun flooded his room, and I had to blink a few times to adjust my eyes to the brightness.

He was on the balcony, looking to the far side of the city. I walked over to stand beside him. My jaw dropped, and I gasped.

The shield over the city was cracked. We stared in disbelief. Holes were spidering as if the shield was made of glass, too.

Looking above the shield, a swirling orange portal appeared. I gaped at the sight of someone falling out of the portal and landing on top of the shield. Orange spells hit the surface of the shield, cracking it at the top. Another hole appeared a few metres from the first ones, and someone jumped through it, floating down into the city.

"Impossible," Kieran muttered.

A black portal opened up above us. We watched as the woman landed on the shield, grinning at us. She hit the shield several times with her black spells until a crack formed. Hitting it one more time, it shattered into another opening. She floated quickly down to a nearby building.

A loud banging on the door pulled our attention away from the invasion. We turned to look across the room. Kieran stood in front of me as if to shield me. He stepped slowly forward.

The banging on the door became louder, and a voice followed. "Kieran!"

"Jake?" I heard Kieran say as he rushed over and opened the door.

Jake stood in the doorway, his face full of worry. His eyes were wide—like he had seen a ghost. Jake caught sight of me standing by the balcony and turned back to Kieran, who was still in his boxers.

"The shield. It's been breached," Jake said in a concerned voice.

"We saw," Kieran muttered.

I walked over and stood beside Kieran. He held my hand and looked at me.

"It's never failed in history," I repeated his own words back to him.

"Now it has," he said, worry evident on his face.

Shattering glass fell onto the balcony; the three of us turned to look. A man landed on the balcony with a thump and instantly put his hand up toward us. His spell let loose, but Kieran was faster. Kieran shielded us and the man's spell dissipated against the shield. Jake threw a lime-green fireball at the Dark Soul Weaver, which tossed him off the balcony.

"We must meet with Demetri," Jake stated urgently.

Kieran nodded just as another bang sounded in the distance.

"Let's hurry," Kieran said as he let go of my hand and rushed to find clothes.

TEN MINUTES LATER, we were in Demetri's room. I felt like I shouldn't be at the council meeting, but Kieran had insisted.

"We need to work quickly to patch the shield," Jake said.

Demetri looked at him. "The only way to fix it is to bring the shield down, then reactivate it."

I looked around at the other council members as an unsettling silence loomed. A woman, a few years older than Demetri, with short black pixie-cut hair, stood in the corner with her arms crossed and lips pursed. A man dressed in a t-shirt and shorts with shaggy sandy-blonde hair leaned on Demetri's desk. Another man, dressed in full white with bright green hair and grey eyes, was playing with a pen in his hands.

"We must create a diversion," Kieran announced, breaking the silence. "Draw them away, so we have time to reactivate it."

"As far as knowledge goes, it takes about an hour to activate it," Demetri replied.

"We've never activated it before?" The woman asked.

"Not for many years." The man with the green hair said.

"So, who is attacking?" I asked.

All eyes turned to me. *Why did I speak?* I bit my lip,

wanting to shrivel away into a plant decoration to camouflage into the room. Kieran squeezed my hand.

Kieran said, "Your parents."

I swallowed. "And how do we distract them?"

The council stared at me. Demetri looked me up and down. His jaw moved as he ground his teeth, his mind ticking.

"If you are really with us, then *you* can be the distraction."

Kieran snapped his head toward Demetri. "What exactly are you implying?"

"She can be the bait to lure them away." Demetri said.

Kieran shook his head and said, "no way."

"We will have a team follow her to ensure her safety." Demetri said.

"That will be extremely dangerous," Kieran said. "If they capture her..."

"They won't." Jake said. "We will ensure there is a strong team with her and bring her back to safety as soon as the shield is back up."

There were murmurs around the council members, but no one objected. The tension in Kieran's muscles radiated down his body into the hand in mine. His jaw clenched. He clearly didn't like this plan.

"Let's move." Demetri said.

Taking a breath, I swallowed again. "So, where am I going then?"

"Are you sure you want to do this?" Kieran said in a

lower voice, worry lines creasing his forehead.

"I have to prove my loyalty, or they will never trust me," I whispered.

All eyes were on us. I had forgotten about their heightened senses—they had heard me. I shifted awkwardly beside Kieran, our arms touching.

"Elvanor Forest," Demetri replied to my question.

"I will go with Kieran to protect her," Jake called.

Demetri turned to Jake. "No. I need you to assist Mae with guarding the platform."

Jake reluctantly nodded.

"Clara will come with us," Kieran said.

"Yes, take Clara." Demetri waved a hand in dismissal. "Go now."

Kieran led me from the room. We could hear Demetri giving orders to the other council members until we rounded the corner and hurried down the ramp.

"Clara will be at the north pylon. That's her guarding point if we're attacked," Kieran said as we picked up the pace.

Other Soul Weavers hurried past us as we got off the ramp; they were muttering to each other about how the shield was falling to pieces. We looked up. The shield was indeed falling to pieces, breaking away from punctured holes. Kieran and I glanced at each other, worry clear on both of our faces.

More Dark Soul Weavers were entering the city as we ran through it; more openings in the shield appeared. We hid behind trees and anything that would hide us to avoid being seen.

As we snuck through Myrdreya, we spotted many Soul Weavers and Dark Soul Weavers fighting in the streets. A young boy, maybe 13 or 14, ran past us and hid behind a glass hedge.

"He's so young," I whispered, tugging on Kieran's shirt.

Kieran nodded. "His parents are here."

I should have known there would be families here. Nodding, I turned my focus back to our mission. We moved as quickly as we could, keeping out of sight as much as possible.

"There she is," Kieran said.

A woman with dark blue short hair stood by the north pylon with another Soul Weaver, a male. She was dressed in flimsy black attire. With unbelievable speed, she threw a golden-yellow ball of energy at a nearby Dark Soul Weaver. He was thrown against a glass wall and knocked unconscious.

Kieran stepped out into the street, heading for the woman. The blue-haired woman had to be Clara.

As I followed, Kieran pivoted, grabbing my waist and pulling me behind him. A Dark Soul Weaver landed where I had been standing a moment ago. Kieran shielded us from the other man's attack; the man's spell disintegrated against Kieran's purple barrier.

A yellow ball flew past us and hit the man in the chest.

He lost his balance and fell over. Clara threw another spell at the man, which paralysed him on the ground.

"He won't stay down for long," Clara shouted.

Kieran grabbed my hand, and we bolted across the street toward Clara. We joined her by the pylon. I looked up; the pylon was so tall that I could barely see the top of it while standing right underneath it.

"We have a mission," Kieran stated.

I brought my attention back to Clara; she had dark blue shoulder length hair, tied back in a plait. Her sleeveless black shirt exposed a large scar, from what looked like a burn, on her left arm.

"Duty calls." Clara glanced at her pylon partner. "You got this pylon under control?"

"No problem," the other Soul Weaver replied.

She nodded. "Take care of yourself."

Clara had barely turned back to us when Kieran started explaining the plan. I zoned out of most of the conversation as I stared at the collapsing shield. Pieces of glass rained down on the city.

"We need to hurry." I said, turning my attention back to Kieran and Clara.

"So, we will follow Trixie closely in case she is in danger," Clara reiterated. "Do you think this will draw them away from Myrdreya?"

"I hope so," Kieran said. "Let's go."

Kieran held my hand and led the way as Clara followed behind us. We ran across the city — out in the open for everyone to see us. I swallowed the uneasy feeling down as my eyes swept over the Dark Soul Weavers, eyeing us.

Clara shouted, "Quickly, let's get to Elvanor forest."

I snapped my eyes to her for a split second. Movement from the Dark Soul Weavers as they advanced on us drew my attention. My heart hastened as Kieran gripped my hand harder and pulled me along with him.

Upon reaching the portal room, Kieran held out his hand and closed his eyes. Purple energy swept out of his fingertips and formed a portal in front of us. Clara stood by the entrance of the room, throwing fireballs at our pursuers.

Kieran placed a soft hand on my cheek. Leaning in, his lips pressed hard against mine.

"We will be right behind you," Kieran said, gazing into my eyes.

I gave him a weak smile and turned toward the portal. Taking a deep breath, I stepped through.

⚜️

THE FOREST WAS eerie, especially walking through it alone. As the bait, I had to make it believable that no one else was with me. Kieran and Clara were high in the trees, watching from above. Somewhere. Knowing they were there made my mission only mildly less daunting.

Autumn had taken hold; I was glad it wasn't the

middle of the night, or else we would freeze out here. I stepped over a tree branch and almost tripped. Gripping onto a tree nearby, I steadied myself.

A stick snapped behind me.

I froze in place.

"Trix."

I knew the voice straight away. Spinning around, I stared directly at Levi.

"What are you doing out here?" he asked.

I watched as he carefully stepped toward me. *What was he doing here?*

"Just taking a walk." I said.

What a stupid lie. Why would anyone be randomly taking a walk in the middle of a forest? I was curious as to why he didn't question me about it. Levi glanced around in the surrounding trees. I followed his gaze.

"Is there something in the trees?" I asked, pretending to be completely alone.

"Please, trust me," Levi said, taking another step closer. "Come with me."

"You know I can't do that, Levi," I replied, shaking my head.

He took another step forward, leaning toward me, and planted his lips on mine before I could object. I pushed him backwards.

"What are you doing?" I barely said when a purple ball of energy erupted in between us.

A transparent shield appeared—separating us.

"Get away from her." A voice followed.

Both Levi and I looked over to where the magic had come from. Kieran stood with his hand still outstretched, only metres away. I walked over to him and stood beside him.

"You're with him now?" Levi looked from Kieran to me.

"And you're with her parents," Kieran stated.

I glanced at Kieran in shock; he avoided my gaze and kept his eyes locked on Levi.

"Tell me that isn't true?" I aimed at Levi.

He looked away, off into the distance of the trees.

"Levi?" I repeated his name, waiting for the answer I dreaded.

"They offered me more power than you Soul Weavers could ever imagine. I took their offer," he stated.

"How *could* you?" I shook my head slowly in disbelief. "That's how you got here...by joining them."

My heart broke. The man I had thought I had known so well was one I really didn't know at all.

"Did you tell him?" Levi said.

I frowned. "Tell him what?"

"About our kiss."

Blood drained from my face. Kieran's eyes were on me, but he said nothing. A stick cracked nearby, drawing our attention.

"What was..." I began.

"They have us surrounded," Kieran casually said as if

he had already known.

"Did you call them?" I threw at Levi.

Levi said nothing. I shook my head. *How could he would betray me like that?* After all that time, all the love he had for me, he could just turn around and deceive me.

"Well done, Levi." A familiar voice spoke behind me.

I spun around to see Delaras leaning casually against a tree trunk in her usual crimson attire. Looking around, I could see at least another three men in the trees; Soul Weavers or not, I wasn't sure. We had not been prepared for an ambush like this. I glanced up in the trees, wondering where Clara was.

"We knew it was you," Kieran shot at the woman.

Delaras tilted her head. "And yet you did nothing."

Kieran clenched his jaw. I glared at Delaras. I had never liked her; there had always been something dark about her, but I never knew what.

"Now, we can do this the easy way or the hard way," Delaras announced, sounding bored.

"The hard way," Kieran said immediately.

I held onto Kieran's hand as I looked at his face. He was focused, not looking at me. I could feel the tension in his muscles, though, as I clung onto his arm. I didn't know how much of that tension was about our situation now or about the kiss.

"Very well," Delaras said and threw her hands up in the air.

Kieran moved quickly. He blocked her red fireball

with a shield. I raised my free hand up, and everyone slowed—everyone except for Kieran and I. Holding his arm had allowed me to not freeze him. I hadn't known if it would work, but I had tried it, anyway.

Kieran glanced at me; he knew what I had done. Without saying a word to each other, we ran.

Hand in hand, we bolted through the forest, bounding over fallen branches and dodging bushes. Clara dropped from the trees beside us.

"They're too fast," Clara said as we ran.

"Keep going!" Kieran urged us.

"How didn't you get slowed?" I asked Clara.

"She was up in the trees. Must have been far enough away." Kieran answered.

Kieran stopped running; he gripped my hand pulling me back as I almost bounded straight past him. He held out his hand and summoned a portal in front of us. I immediately recognised the glass platform in Myrdreya.

Kieran nodded to Clara to go through first. As soon as Clara had gone out of sight, I gripped Kieran's hand tighter, and we stepped forward.

Something hard grabbed me on the shoulder, pulling me backwards.

I yelled out in fright.

Kieran jerked in my grip as he turned around to see the man holding onto me. Kieran tried to pull me out of the man's hold, but someone else hit him hard in the chest. I couldn't hold on—our hands parted.

"KIERAN!" I screamed as his body fell backward.

I caught a quick glance of horror on his face before he, and the portal, vanished.

Nineteen

I FELL BACKWARDS THROUGH MY portal and landed hard on my back. Jumping to my feet, my portal vanished in front of my eyes.

"TRIXIE!" I yelled.

I knew it was useless; there was no way she could hear me. I shook my head in disbelief. *Fuck. How did our plan go so wrong?* My body trembled.

"No, no, no, no," I muttered.

"Kieran?" Clara said. "Wha-a-t happened? Where's Trixie?"

Clara stood on the bridge, waiting for me.

Ignoring Clara, I raced straight past her. I could hear her footsteps following me as I bolted to the portal room. If I didn't need my energy, I would have just opened a portal back straight away, but I needed it to fight to get her back. Opening the portal back to Myrdreya had already weakened me.

"I need a portal back!" I yelled as I entered the room.

Heads turned and stared at me. I glared around the room. Clara stood beside me. My breathing was uneven, as if I was out of breath—except I knew I couldn't be. I was hyperventilating. Panicking.

"What happened? What are you doing here?" Mae, the other portal keeper, questioned.

"They've taken her. We have to get her back!" I blurted through my breaths.

Mae stared at me. I heard footsteps behind me and spun around to face Demetri.

"Demetri..." I said.

"It's too late," Demetri said, his eyes unfocused. "They've already taken another portal away."

"No!" I stepped toward him. "We can't just *give* up. You said we would protect her."

"They got what they wanted...for now," he continued. "It will be near impossible to track them."

"Well, I have to try." I stalked straight past him, hands clenched into fists at my sides.

"Where are you going, Kieran?" Demetri said.

"To find Trixie," I stated as I exited the portal room, not looking back.

"It's pointless."

"I don't care." I bellowed over my shoulder.

No matter the cost, I had to find her. Running footsteps sounded to my right. I looked over to see Clara had caught up to me.

"We will find her." Clara said.

She grabbed my wrist and stopped me from walking. I glared at her.

"Now is not the time." She said. "We can't just storm off looking for her. Who knows where she could be? We have to be strategic about this."

Gritting my teeth, I sighed. She was right. We could walk right into a trap if we're not careful.

Twenty

TRIXIE

"ARE YOU SURE WE WEREN'T followed?"

"Yes. I scouted the area and saw no one."

"Good."

"Is she awake yet?"

"No."

I kept my eyes shut tight. I vaguely heard the conversation nearby, but didn't know who the voices belonged to. *Where am I?* Dirt and mould reached my nostrils. I fought the urge to screw up my face from the smell.

My head pounded. *Argh, this headache. Had I fallen? Did they knock me out?* I didn't remember falling or getting hit.

The portal. Kieran. Yelling.

The memory came back to me.

I tried to move my hand, but it wouldn't listen to my instruction. Dread washed over me — paralysed. My heart pounded behind my rib cage as I panicked silently.

"She's been unconscious for a long time." I heard someone say.

"Are you sure she's a Soul Weaver?" Another voice asked.

"Most definitely." A woman said.

Delaras. My blood boiled. *How could she betray her own kind like that? Her friends.*

Footsteps drew my attention from my thoughts. It sounded like they were walking on dirt and gravel. *Where on earth am I?* Keeping my eyes closed, I continued to listen.

"What are you going to do with her?" A familiar male's voice spoke from across the room.

Levi. I wanted to spit his name, but my lips wouldn't move. Fury built up inside of my soul. *Betrayer! Trust him? He left to keep me safe? What a load of bullshit.*

"I don't believe that was part of the deal," Delaras snapped.

"No, I-I was just w-wondering." Levi stuttered.

"Wonder elsewhere." Delaras spat.

He had turned me in without even knowing what they

would do with me. *How could he do that to me, after the feelings we had for each other?*

If my body would move, it would shake with fear. My insides trembled, but I wasn't physically shaking—I didn't think.

More footsteps and another voice came into earshot.

"She would like to speak with her—alone."

"She's not awake yet," Delaras said.

"She will wake her," the other person replied; I wasn't sure if the person was male or female.

"She was knocked out," Delaras said. "You can't just wake her."

The other person sighed and sounded like they had walked away. So they *had* knocked me out. That explains why my head hurt so much. More footsteps. *How many people were here?* The footsteps stopped, and the air was eerily quiet for a moment.

"There was no need to knock her out," a woman said.

The sound of her voice sent chills down my spine. I risked a peak. Slowly, I opened my eyes the tiniest amount; just enough so I could glimpse at my mother.

She looked very different from how I remembered her. Last time I saw her, she wore skirts and floral tops with long blonde hair tied in ponytails. Now, she was dressed in slimming black leather pants and a jacket with gold trimming. Her hair was in a pixie-cut and had been dyed black. She was barely recognisable except for her eyes— my eyes.

I hadn't seen or heard from her in years, and now she was talking as though I was no one important to her. Because I wasn't. If I had been, she wouldn't have left me behind. My mother wouldn't have left me as a child to learn how to survive on my own. She wouldn't have left me to suffer from depression and anxiety on my own. I wouldn't have become depressed in the first place. My parents had left me alone in the world. My parents' abandonment had caused me to lose my soul. They had broken me.

"There was no way she was going to come easily," Delaras said.

Peering through the thin slit in my eyelids, I saw my mother glance over at Levi.

"You did well." She said.

He averted his eyes toward me. I quickly shut my eyes tight. Listening, I could hear the disappointment in his voice.

"Thank you." He said.

"Oh please. If it wasn't for me, we wouldn't have captured her." Delaras' voice followed.

"It was Levi's distraction that gave you the chance to even get close to her," my mother said sternly.

I could imagine the anger planted on Delaras' face, but I didn't risk peeking again. Light footsteps circled around me. My mother, I assumed.

"Leave us," my mother commanded loudly.

There were footsteps and ruffled dirt as several pairs

of feet left the room. It became very silent and eerie. I focused on keeping my breathing even and not moving my eyes.

"I know you're awake," she said.

I stayed silent.

"You used to pretend to be asleep a lot when you were a child," she said. "You were very convincing, but I always knew you were awake."

I clearly couldn't keep up with the ruse. I opened my eyes and focused on her, still not being able to move my limbs. Swallowing, I stared at the face of my mother with hatred. Her mouth perked up at the corner as she stared into my eyes.

She flicked her wrist, and my lips parted. I sucked in air through my mouth. She had given the use of my mouth back. Her smile grew wider. It wasn't the smile I remembered — it was more wicked and cunning. She was *not* my mother.

"Hi, Trixie."

After all these years, all she could say to me was 'hi?' My blood boiled through my veins; the emotions surging through my body. I was angry. No, I was *furious.*

"So you're a Soul Weaver," she said.

"So are you, it seems," I mumbled.

She smiled smugly. "Yes, I am."

"What do you want with me?"

"You're my daughter. I want you by my side like your father," she said — like it was an obvious answer.

"Yet, you left me alone as a child," I spat.

"You were exactly that, a child." She raised her eyebrows. "You couldn't have come with us unless you were older."

"So you abandoned your own child for what...power?"

"No, not abandon. We left you to protect you until you were old enough."

"To protect me?" I said, anger boiling in my blood. "And how exactly did you protect me? I was sent off to an orphanage, then I had to find a job and live on my own so I could get out of that disastrous place. And where were you? In this world, forgetting about me."

"No...we never forgot about you. We love you."

"Well, you've got an interesting way of showing it!" I snapped.

My mother sighed. "I know it's hard to understand..."

"Soul Hunters came after me. They killed Kiarra." I said, staring deep into her eyes.

"A tragic death." She said, no hint of pity in her cold voice.

I chewed my cheek and stayed silent. *To protect me... what bullshit.* There was no way I would betray Kieran — or anyone from Myrdreya. They were becoming my family now. My parents were *not* my family. Not anymore.

"Stay with me, Trixie," my mother said. "I can give you power beyond your dreams."

"Power?" I said. "Are you that oblivious to who I am that you think I want *power*? You can give me nothing I want."

Empty words. I could see straight through her. Leaving your child to protect them was not protecting them. *Give me power?* I didn't want power. I wanted love. I wanted respect. It was clear I would get neither from my parents.

She titled her head. "I can give you more than those Soul Weavers in Myrdreya could ever give you."

"I highly doubt you could give me anything compared to the kindness they have shown me," I said. "*You* abandoned me, remember?"

My mother paced back and forth for a minute in silence. All this time. And all she wanted to give me was power.

When she stopped moving, she looked at me out of the corner of her eye.

"I can see you will never be on our side," she said.

I stared at her.

She slowly stepped around me.

"I'm sorry, Trixie." She stopped at my right side. "But you've left me no choice."

Turning my head, the only part of my body I could move, I looked directly into her eyes. There was no sadness there; she wasn't even remotely sorry. She put her hand out toward me.

I swallowed. If my muscles could move, my body

would have been trembling. This was it—she was going to murder her own daughter. I wouldn't even get to say goodbye to my friends, to Kieran.

"What are you doing to her?" Levi's voice said.

I flicked my head toward the doorway to see Levi staring at my mother. She started muttering some words I couldn't understand. Bright light brought my attention back to her. Swirls of red magic floated around her hand, and it was pointing at my face.

"What are you…" I couldn't finish my sentence.

The swirls hit me in the face, and white light took over my vision. I stood frozen in place. Hearing and seeing nothing but white, I panicked. My heart pounded hard in my chest; my whole body shook inside. After what felt like a long time, the panic in my bones subsided.

As the light faded, my vision came back, and my muscles relaxed. Levi stood in front of me, staring blankly. My mother stood next to him.

"Trixie?" Levi said. "Are you okay?"

I frowned at him, dazed, as I pushed myself up to stand. "Yes, of course. Why wouldn't I be?"

His eyes were wide as he stared at me. I looked around the room I was in. *How did I get here? Where was I?* I spotted my mother standing nearby.

"Mum," I mumbled, "Oh, Mum, I've missed you."

Something inside my body jolted—did I just say I *missed* her?

"Oh, baby girl, I've missed you too." She threw her

arms around me, squeezing me tightly.

I returned her embrace. Confusion wrapped around me. *How did I just go from hating her for abandoning me to missing her?* The truth was, I didn't miss her.

"Come. Your father will be so pleased to see you again."

I glanced at Levi. He hadn't moved. He stared at me warily with a look I had never seen on his face before.

"Come, dear."

My attention was brought back to my mother, who was standing by the door.

I followed her. I didn't know why I was so freely following her, or why Levi was here with my parents. I couldn't stop myself; it was like I had no control over my actions. She led me down a corridor that was dirtier and darker than the room we had been in.

After what felt like half an hour of trudging along dark corridors and twisting staircases, we entered a larger room. This room was very well lit—the walls and ceiling were high above us. A few people occupied a long table that sat in the middle of the room. Heads turned, and I spotted my father immediately.

He still had the same dark hair, but he somehow looked different.

"Dad!" I heard myself chime, startling myself. "I have missed you."

I frowned at myself—more words I hadn't expected to say. I quickly hid my confusion and smiled at him.

I saw him glance at my mother questioningly before turning back to me.

"It's terrific to see you," he said. "It's been so long."

"Too long," I said. *Not long enough,* I thought.

My father beamed at me as he stood and welcomed me into his arms. I embracing him, even though all I really wanted to do was push him away and run.

"Please join us for lunch." My father said.

Lunch? It had been midday when I was with Kieran when the attack started. *Was that yesterday? How long had I been knocked out?*

My legs carried me like they weren't even mine. I seated myself next to my father.

"Trixie, how have you been?" My father asked.

"Good, Dad," I said. *No, I haven't! I've been miserable my whole life because of you two.*

"What did you do for a living?"

"I was a freelance editor for novels." *Was?* Oh, no. I had forgotten about my job.

"I am sorry about your friend," he said, his eyes flicked to my mother momentarily.

"Thank you; it was a tragedy."

A tragedy? What was wrong with me? I was talking like Kiarra's death meant nothing. Wait...I never told them about her murder. *Were they behind it?* They had Levi on their side. *Were there other Soul Hunters on their side too? Did they order that man to murder her?* Anger boiled in my blood.

My heartbeat quickened, but my mouth was smiling like there was nothing wrong with the situation. Yet, everything was wrong with this situation. I screamed in my mind, but no words formed.

Twenty-One

TRIXIE

I FELT LIKE A PRISONER—although I didn't understand why. A guard was always stationed outside my room and followed me everywhere I went. I didn't know how long I had been down in this cave; my skin hadn't felt the warmth of sunlight in at least a few days.

When I had questioned my mother about my personal guard two days ago, she told me it was for my safety. *Why did I need a guard for safety in a tunnel that was clearly already heavily guarded?* I doubted anyone could find us here.

I had searched for a ray of sunlight to get some fresh air, but I only found cave after cave. At one point, I thought I was just walking in circles. I wondered how long this cave had been here; it looked man-made but also ancient. It must be a thousand years old.

The cave had small rooms, large rooms, and hallways of bedrooms. Each bedroom—or cave room, as I liked to call them—had a clothing wardrobe, a chair, and a double bed. My room was at the end of one of the hallways.

Leaving my cave room, I walked down the tunnel; the guard followed me without a word. I thought I would get used to having someone follow me everywhere, but I silently groaned every time I left my room.

I rounded a corner and almost smashed into Levi's shoulder.

"Trixie!" He stared at me, surprised.

"Levi, sorry." I apologised hastily, jumping backwards.

He shook his head. "No need to apologise. No harm done."

He smiled at me with the dazzling smile that had won my heart many years ago. I looked him up and down; he was more muscular than I remembered. He was wearing denim jeans and a black t-shirt with an unzipped black jacket. His ice-blue eyes glowed in the light from the cave.

"I've missed you." The words were out of my mouth before I could stop them. *Why did I say that?*

He stared into my eyes. His expression unreadable.

"I have missed you, too." He took a step closer.

I could smell his cologne and the mint on his breath. Feeling mesmerised, I stared back into his eyes. I closed what remained of the gap between us, pressing my body against his. My arms wrapped around the back of his neck. His hands gripped my hips as he leaned down toward me.

His mouth was on mine. Allowing him to engulf my mind, I leaned into his muscular body. I didn't understand what was happening, but I didn't care. I longed for his touch, and it seemed he felt the same.

He broke away, breathing hard.

"Did you want to get out of the corridor?" He said.

I nodded in agreement. His hand gripped mine as he led me down the tunnel. My assigned guard was following us. We stopped outside a door, and Levi opened it. He stepped aside to allow me to enter and followed me in as he closed the door behind him—locking the guard out.

"He will probably wait outside for me," I said.

"I don't doubt it." Levi walked across the room to me, and we locked into another embrace.

It felt so natural, like we had no time apart. He slid his hands up my body, pulling my shirt over my head and throwing it to the floor. He looked down at my basic black bra.

"You always wear black."

"Black is elegant." I shrugged.

His mouth twisted into a smile before his lips were on mine again. *What am I doing? How is this evening happening? Why have I let myself fall straight back into his arms again?*

There was a bang on the door, and we broke apart. I heard Levi sigh as he went for the door. I quickly grabbed my shirt from the floor and pulled it back on.

"Yes?" Levi said as the door swung open. He quickly added, "My Lady."

My mother stared across the room at me; she noticed I was straightening my shirt and looked at Levi.

"You know it's not real," she muttered to Levi.

I narrowed my eyes, watching Levi. *What did she mean by that?* Levi seemed to understand as he nodded, disappointment clear on his face.

"Come, Trixie." My mother addressed me.

I walked across the room; I still didn't understand why I was in this tunnel obeying my mother so readily. *What was going on with me? Had I lost my mind?*

I exited Levi's room and waited for my mother to lead the way. I watched as she leant in toward Levi. I focused my senses and pushed my hearing to listen.

"Don't blow it," my mother whispered sternly.

"I…" Levi began.

"You know she's not herself."

Not herself?

Were they talking about me? I didn't feel like myself. *Nothing was making sense. I'm saying things I don't mean, and*

I can't seem to control my actions. What was wrong with me?

My mother left Levi standing by the door and came toward me. She strolled straight past me, and I turned to follow. We entered a large room, and I saw my father and Delaras sitting at the table in the middle of the room. The same room I had seen my father in days ago.

"Trixie, please join us." My father indicated to a chair next to him.

I obediently sat down next to him before I could even consider my actions. My mother followed and sat across the table from me.

"So, can we trust that you are on our side?" my father said.

"Of course, father." I said. *What? I'm not on their side!*

"In a few days, we are going to portal to Myrdreya. But only you can get us in," he explained. "They wouldn't have stopped your ability to portal in yet, so you must portal us all there."

I nodded. "Sure."

No! What are you doing? I yelled at myself in my head. *I can't betray the Soul Weavers like this.*

"Whatever you need." I heard come out of my mouth.

Okay, now I knew something was terribly wrong. *Why was I saying the complete opposite of what I wanted to say?* Horror erupted through my blood. *Oh, no – the spell – she's controlling me.*

I had lost control of my free will—of my soul. I would betray Kieran, and I couldn't do a thing about it.

Twenty-Two

KIERAN

*I*T WAS THE MIDDLE OF the night, and I was too restless to sleep. My mind too focused on Trixie. *Where was she? Was she alright? What were they doing to her?* I had to find her. I wouldn't forgive myself if something happened to her.

I climbed out of bed and dressed, pulling on my black fighting gear and shoes. Opening my bedroom door quietly, I peered out into the hallway. It was empty. I left my room, shutting the door behind me, and soundlessly made my way across the mansion.

Turning the corner, I almost walked straight into a muscular man. Jake.

"Kieran," he said in surprise; then his eyes wandered over me and narrowed. "Where are you going?"

"Don't try to stop me," I said.

"Shall I rephrase...where are *we* going?"

I raised my eyebrows.

"I will not let you rescue her by yourself. You will need a team," he answered my unspoken question.

I sighed. "Thank you."

He bowed his head. "It's the least I can do for what you have been doing for me."

I nodded.

"We need Clara." I began leading us down the hallway toward my partner's bedroom.

I knocked on her door quietly, careful not to wake up anyone else in the nearby rooms. She didn't answer. I held out a hand and focused on the doorknob. After a moment, purple swirls licked the invisible door lock, and it clicked.

Jake pushed the door open, and we quietly stepped inside, closing the door behind us.

"Clara," I whispered.

No answer. I stepped closer to her bed; she was sleeping peacefully.

"Clara," I said louder as I touched her arm.

I jumped back as she swung her fists at me; one hand with a blade protruding.

"Wow, easy. It's Kieran," I blurted.

Clara sighed and let her arms relax, placing the dagger on her bedside table.

"What are you doing here?" Clara whispered as she glanced around her bedroom, her eyes settling on Jake.

"Hi, Clara," Jake said politely, still by the door.

"Jake." She nodded her head to him before turning back to me. "What's going on?"

"We're going to find her," I answered. "I was hoping you would join..."

I didn't even finish my sentence before Clara started climbing out of bed.

"Let me get dressed," she said, walking over to her closet.

Jake and I turned around, facing the door. A few moments passed, and Clara joined us by the door in full black attire. I turned to look at her as she clasped her dagger to her belt.

"Alright, let's go." She said.

We swung by Jake's room so he could change, and then we headed out of the mansion, passing no one. It quite surprised me we didn't see at least one other guard walking around.

"So, do you know where she might be?" Clara asked as we discreetly walked through Myrdreya toward the portal room.

I shook my head. I didn't have a clue where she had been taken.

She stopped walking. "How are we supposed to find

her if you have no idea where she is? She could be anywhere by now."

"I thought we would go back to where they took her and see if we can track them," I answered as I continued walking forward.

Clara caught up with us quickly. "You know the chances of finding her..."

"I know, but I have to try," I said. I didn't want to hear that we wouldn't find her.

"We are with you," Jake stated, placing a hand on my shoulder.

I nodded to him in acknowledgement as we entered the portal room.

They were my best friends; I knew I could count on them. Without them, the chance of finding her was slim. I wasn't a tracker, but Clara was. Living with myself if something happened to her—I couldn't even think about that. I refused to think that she was gone, that I would never lay my eyes on her beautiful blue ones again.

Twenty-Three

"**T**RIX..."

I vaguely heard my name being whispered.

"Trixie, wake up."

I rolled over and shooed the voice away with a hand.

"Trixie!" the voice called louder while shaking my shoulder.

Snapping my eyes open, I rolled back over and stared up at the figure towering over me. I gasped and bolted upright, pushing the being away in the darkness.

"Trix, it's just me."

Levi. I slumped back down into my pillow and pulled the covers up to my neck. I shivered in the cold, damp air.

"Wha're you doin'?" My words slurred. *Why was he waking me up in the dead of night? What time was it? It was confusing being in the dark cave.*

"It's time," he answered.

"Time for what?" I mumbled, rubbing my eyes.

"For Myrdreya."

I froze. Nauseous, I moved a hand to my stomach. Looking up at him, his expression was unreadable. I couldn't tell if he was on my parents' side or mine — the side I truly believed in.

※ ◉ ※

STANDING IN A dark tunnel lit by candles, I waited with Levi as my parents joined us.

"Ready?" my mother asked as they stopped in front of us.

Yawning, I replied, "Yes, Mother."

No! You're not ready. Should never be prepared for being a traitor. I subconsciously snarled to myself. I showed them no sign of distress — not because I didn't want to show it, but because I had no control over anything.

"They are waiting for us in the hall," my father said. He indicated with his head toward the tunnel.

They? Who are they talking about? My parents turned and led the way toward the hall my father mentioned.

Levi and I followed obediently. Our boots scuffed the dirt and our footsteps echoed off the walls, the only thing breaking the eerie silence. My feet carried me forward, but I wanted to run in the opposite direction. My mind screamed, but my limbs wouldn't obey.

As we walked through the arched doorway into the hall. My eyes widened in horror. My face restored itself in an instant against my will.

Ancient pillars stood around the bland room, holding the high ceiling up. Candles lined the walls and pillars lighting the massive room in front of me. It wasn't the look of the hall that horrified me, though.

Gathered in the hall were hundreds of people; a mixture of Soul Hunters and Dark Soul Weavers. It was a sea of black and red; the only difference between them was the hunters had swords on their belt or backs, or they had a bow slung over their shoulders with a quiver full of arrows.

I glanced sideways at Levi, who stood beside me. He, too, wore the same black and red gear. He had a sword sheathed on his belt. I looked down at myself and bile rose in my throat. Black and red.

No, no, no, no.

I looked like them. I looked like a Dark Soul Weaver.

A buzz of sound filled the air as they chatted amongst themselves, but silence quickly swept across the room as my mother entered from another door off to the left. I stared at my mother—she was wearing black and dark purple. All eyes on her.

"My friends," she opened her arms wide toward the crowd. "Today, we finally take it!"

The horde in front of her cheered. My heart was throbbing behind my ribs, yet I couldn't will my legs to run.

"My daughter." She pointed at me. "Will open the portal to get us there."

An uproar of cheering filled the hall. I looked around at the staring, cheering faces. *How could that many people follow my mother?* I feared what might happen today. Scared of what Kieran would think of me when we entered the city. I couldn't stop it from happening. My mind was my own, but my body was...controlled.

"It's time, Trixie." She looked at me, her eyes piercing and expectant. "Summon the portal into Myrdreya."

No! I screamed, but no words came out. My hands rose in front of me, completely submissive to her, no matter how hard I tried to stop them. I pulled at my muscles, but they wouldn't listen. Turquoise swirls erupted from my fingers, growing and forming a portal. The swirls inside the portal were frosted like glass. My heart sank.

"Begin," my mother announced, evil laughter escaping her lips as they curled in triumph.

I stepped backwards as everyone else rushed forward, diving into my portal. I wanted to hide and cry. If I had control of my body, I would have a waterfall of tears rolling down my cheeks. I helplessly stood by as I watched them step through my portal into the city I adored.

Once the majority had gone through, my father stepped through without a glance in my direction. Levi smiled weakly at me before leaving my side and following the rest. I didn't understand why Levi was doing this. *How could he betray me like this?*

Everyone had gone through except for my mother and me.

"Our turn," my mother stated as she gripped my arm, pulling me forward.

There was no point in struggling. My limbs wouldn't obey if I tried. At least we were going back to where I wanted to be. I took a breath and shut my eyes as she dragged me through the portal with her.

᠉᠉᠉ ◉ ᠊᠊᠊

SQUEEZING MY EYES shut, I blocked out the sunlight. I could still see the blinding light through my eyelids. Slowly, bit by bit, I allowed my eyes to crack open and squinted through the light—brightness I hadn't seen in many days. My arm had been released, and I immediately wanted to jump back through my portal and hide.

I turned around, squinting to find my portal—but it was already gone. Even if the portal had been there still, there was no way my body would move toward it.

Swallowing, I looked over my shoulder at the battle that had unfolded.

Myrdreya. The glass city that I adored was breaking apart. Holes in the sides of buildings, trees all but fallen over and smashed apart. Soul Hunters and Dark Soul Weavers surrounded the platform I was standing on. All I could see was magic erupting from hands and blasting at the Soul Weavers. Orbs of colour flying in all directions. I looked up — the shield was intact, they must have successfully mended it while I was gone.

My legs carried me forward. *What was happening?* The urge built up inside me to join in; I ran forward with my hand outstretched and blasted a Soul Weaver off his feet. I stared in horror at the man I had attacked, although my facial expression hadn't changed.

I couldn't control my desire to fight against those that I had only recently been in alliance with. I started yelling at myself in my mind. *What am I doing? Stop! These people are my friends.*

I threw another magic blast at a nearby Soul Weaver. He fell backwards and stared at me in shock. *Stop! They are not my enemy. What is wrong with me?* I continued having a battle of my own, inside of my head — but it was a losing battle.

I followed the other Soul Hunters and Dark Soul Weavers further into Myrdreya. We attacked everyone in our path. I didn't know what the plan of this battle actually was — well, that was until my mother spoke from beside me.

"Good, Trixie. Let's take Myrdreya together."

I swallowed as my feet carried me forward. They were going to take over the floating city. My mind wanted to run and hide, ashamed of what I was doing. My body wanted to fight, and I couldn't stop it. I felt lost and miserable. *How could this happen to me? Why were my parents controlling me?*

My father pushed magic out from his hands; it was orange, and it formed a semicircle dome in front of him. As it grew larger, it began shielding us from the Soul Weaver's retort. I watched as the Soul Hunters began striking my friends through the orange shield with long whips; I realised they were, in fact, taser weapons. The Soul Weavers were being electrocuted and fell to the ground one by one.

I couldn't do anything but watch my friends fall. A sinking feeling in my stomach overcame me. Outside, I was their enemy, but inside I wanted to help the Soul Weavers. I had no way of communicating with them. To tell them my parents forced me to attack them, to show I was on their side.

My father slowly pushed the shield forward so we could keep moving through the city. Minute by minute, we drove the Soul Weavers back further into the city. I caught Demetri's eye, and he shook his head at me. My body reacted; a smirk twisted at my mouth.

Stop it! I would never react this way. They must despise me so much right now. I had betrayed them, and

I had lost all of their trust. I yelled at myself, but it was no use.

Kieran. *What would he think of me?* My mind cried, but no tears formed. I wanted to find the closest edge of the floating city and jump.

Twenty-Four

KIERAN

I STOOD BY JAKE ON the ground as we scouted the area near Trixie's house. Clara was in the canopy of the trees overlooking the area. We had found no trace of her. We had tried the place they had taken her from, but there was nothing.

"How are we going to find her when there is no trace of her?" Jake commented.

"I don't know, but I have to try." I said.

There was movement up ahead. A swirl of a portal appeared, it was faded — the other end of it. Someone was coming through. Jake and I jumped behind a nearby bush and watched as a woman clambered out of the portal.

I peeked through the leaves.

"Kyra?"

The short woman with sandy blonde hair looked over toward me. Oh, right. I stood up to expose myself. Jake followed my league.

"You boys better get back to Myrdreya. We're being invaded," Kyra replied, her hazel eyes flashing between us. "Where is Clara?"

"Where do you think?" Jake said sarcastically.

I pointed up into the trees.

Kyra nodded. "Of course. Well, call for her and get back to Myrdreya."

"What is going on?" I asked.

"Your *girlfriend* let them in." Kyra stated in a heavy tone.

I blinked, staring. Words escaped me. I couldn't comprehend what she had just said. I had to have misheard.

"Pardon?"

"You heard me." Kyra said. "*She* let *them* in."

MY HEART SANK, like a ship in the depths of an ocean.

I couldn't believe what I was seeing. Trixie was fighting—against us. No, this couldn't be. I stared in horror as she blasted a Soul Weaver backwards off their feet.

Jake appeared next to me. "They've turned her against us."

"No..." I shook my head. "There's no way she would..."

The woman I watched right now wasn't Trixie. The way she moved and her expressions weren't anything like the Trixie I knew. She couldn't be. She didn't even glance my way. If this was Trixie, she would be looking for me, but this woman was foreign.

"Kieran—." Jake started.

"What can we do?" I questioned urgently.

Movement caught my eye, and I hastily looked to my left. A man was hovering behind a tree. I stared at him, and he stared back. Levi—I recognised him immediately. My jaw clenched as I strode over to him. Levi stood still, except for a flinch as I neared him. He made no move to run.

"WHAT DID YOU DO TO HER?" I yelled, grabbing him by the throat, thrusting him against the tree.

"It—wasn't—me," Levi choked.

I glared at him, pinning him against the bark. Jake was beside me, ready to defend me.

"Please—I have come to tell you—."

"Tell me what?" I spat, interrupting his pleading.

He coughed. "I will—if you—let me—go."

I eyed him warily. Jake held up his hand, yellow swirls

forming in his palm. I glanced at him. Jake nodded; we silently agreed to be ready to attack. I slowly released him.

Levi coughed again, massaging his throat. "She's not herself."

I narrowed my eyes. "What do you mean?"

Levi indicated to Jake's glowing hands, "that's not necessary."

"Get on with it." I growled, anger boiling up inside me.

"Her parents...they put a spell on her to control her. Well...her mother did." He paused as he looked from Jake to me. "She's got no control over her actions."

Jake and I glanced at each other. Furious, I stared back at Levi; then I pounced at him, knocking him back against the tree.

"I've got nothing to do with it!" Levi quickly threw at me.

I narrowed my eyes, studying his face carefully. Jake put a hand on my shoulder, and I looked at him.

"He's telling the truth." Jake stated.

I growled. "Tell us what happened."

"After she captured, she was bound in a cave. She couldn't move. Julianne released her mouth so she could speak. I came in and..." Levi's voice trailed off.

"And what?"

"And Julianne cast a spell on her. Next thing I knew, Trixie sat up and acted like she *missed* her mother."

"How do we break the spell?" I demanded.

He shook his head. "All I know…is they told me to keep you away from her. They said: *You're her weakness.*"

I released him again, gazing off into the distance.

"I don't know what they meant by that, but I've seen how she looks at you. You mean a lot to her, and I think you have to be the one to save her," Levi said.

I could hear the sadness in his voice; he clearly still cared for her. He appeared to be regretting his words as they left his mouth.

"I'm her weakness…" I muttered to myself. "What does that mean…"

I didn't understand, but I knew I needed to save Trixie. I had to resurrect her soul. Losing her wasn't an option. She was lost in her own body, and I had to save her.

"Why did you tell me this?" I asked, glaring at him.

"I've loved her for years. I can't watch her be controlled," he choked out. "I-I believe you can free her."

I considered his words for a moment.

Reaching my hands up on either side of my head, I focused carefully and closed my eyes. Purple swirls licked out of my fingertips and enveloped my head. I repeated the words in my mind as I opened my eyes. I watched the purple cover my sight. A moment later, the swirls were gone. Jake glanced at me. His eyes wandered over my face, but he said nothing. Levi stared at me, his mouth hanging open. He shifted backward.

"Protection spell," I explained to Levi.

He nodded, but still stared at me with his mouth hanging.

"We need to find her," I said.

I gripped the tree as I peered around it toward the battle, my grip tight enough on the bark that it had left an impression on my skin.

Spells cast back and forth between the Soul Weavers and Dark Soul Weavers as I scanned the mass of fighters, searching for her. Everywhere I looked, there was a band of black and red fighting against us. Soul Weavers ducked and dodged fireballs and threw back some of their own. It was a dizzying mix of colours.

And then I saw her. She moved with purpose alongside the Dark Soul Weavers, her long blonde hair streaming behind her.

"They won't let you get close to her. They know the weakness of the spell," Levi said, peeking around the tree trunk.

"You can lure her away, toward us," Jake chimed in.

Reluctantly, I took my eyes from Trixie and glanced at Jake before looking at Levi questioningly. Levi stared back at me, a strange expression of contemplation on his face. He appeared to be lost in thought.

"I think I can do that. She will follow me," he agreed confidently.

I nodded. "We will wait here. Make sure her parents don't see."

Levi nodded again and turned. I reached out and gripped his arm. He snapped his head back to me with wide eyes.

"Cross us," I said through gritted teeth, "and I'll make sure you regret it."

Levi took a breath and nodded. I released his arm.

Twenty-Five

TRIXIE

RAPPED IN A TRANCE, I shuffled along blindly. My legs forced me forward, following the crowd of Dark Soul Weavers and Hunters. I felt like a zombie; disconnected from my body. My mother had me in her clutches and was forcing me forward. The iron cage of her gaze locked onto mine, and no matter how much I yelled inside my mind, I couldn't break free of the spell. She had a deep hold on me, and I did not know how I would escape.

Staring ahead, I was horrified at the chaos growing.

Fireballs flew this way and that way, a sea of colours in the crowd of black-clad people.

Levi emerged from between some glass buildings to my right and joined my side. I glanced at him. His eyes flitted from one person to another, as if searching for an escape route. He turned to me, leaning toward my ear.

"I saw someone run off in between those buildings. Do you want to help me find them?" he asked.

"Sure." My voice escaped my lips, but I frowned internally.

I stumbled away from the war zone, my mind in a daze as I pulled myself away from the chaos. He walked ahead of me, between two glass buildings. I looked back, searching the crowd for my mother. She hadn't noticed we had left.

"Come quick, over this way," Levi hushed.

I hastened my steps as I walked over to him. I thought he could have been on my side, but now I wasn't so sure. Yet, he seemed quite tense, worry lines on his brow and in his eyes.

He led me toward a tree trunk in between the buildings; the battle was now almost out of our sight.

"He went this way," Levi said, standing by a large tree.

Following him over to the tree, I froze. My muscles locked up, feet rooted to the ground. Kieran and Jake stepped out like prowling panthers.

KIERAN!

I screamed, but no words escaped my lips.

KIERAN!

I tried again, but it was no use. I could only shout in my head. My hand flew up in front of me automatically. *No, please, no.* I couldn't stop myself. Turquoise grew at my fingertips and a spell erupted. Before it hit Kieran in the chest, he deflected my attack, throwing his hand up as a small shield grew out of his palm.

"Trixie, it's me." Kieran's voice was warming.

I know it's you. Help me, please.

I couldn't speak. As much as I tried to form the words on the tip of my tongue, nothing came out—it was like my lips had been sealed shut. Screaming at myself inside, but totally emotionless on the outside—I stood there. *How can I tell him what's happened?*

"I'm here to help you," he said, his hands up in front of his chest. "Please, this isn't you."

"He knows you're being controlled. I told him," Levi said.

"What are you talking about? I am not being controlled." My words were sharp, but my inner turmoil was deafening.

"Trixie, please remember who you are," Kieran said.

"She is who she is meant to be." A stern voice came from behind us.

I didn't need to turn around to know who it belonged to. My mother stalked past me and threw a glare at Levi, then looked at me.

"My daughter, come. We need you back with everyone else."

"No! Why are you doing this?" Kieran shouted. "She is not a puppet!"

I glanced at each of their faces—from Kieran to Levi, to Jake, and to my mother. I stood in between them, still frozen in place. My expression was unreadable, but my thoughts were chaotic. I wanted to tell Kieran that I understood him, that I was still here in my head.

"It's time for you and your Soul Weaver's hand over Myrdreya and leave," she spat at him.

No, fight back, Kieran! I wanted to say to him, but no words formed.

"And let you destroy everything we are here to protect?" Kieran returned darkly. "Never."

"I guess it will be the hard way, then." She raised her hands and sparks crackled at her fingertips.

Kieran and Jake raised their hands up in defence, but neither was fast enough. A spell hit Kieran in the arm, and his sleeve seared. Levi jumped backwards, out of harm's way. Jake stepped forward to retaliate with a fireball, but with a swish of my mother's hand, she batted away Jake's fireball as if it was a feather. She then launched him skyward before he crashed into a nearby wall. Glancing at Jake, I saw him rolling over to stand.

Kieran didn't spare a glimpse at Jake. He threw fireball after fireball toward my mother, but again, she easily deflected. Her expression turned fierce as she stepped to the side and pushed both her hands out in front of her. Two fireballs grew and rocketed toward Kieran.

My hands automatically flew up as I yelled, "NO!"

The sound of my own voice startled me; I had spoken with my own volition. Kieran spun and ducked to dodge the double fireballs. My mother was casting another fireball as turquoise energy burst out of my fingers and exploded. For a moment, I didn't know what had happened. My body was heavy from exhaustion. I looked around.

"Trixie?" Kieran's voice whispered longingly.

"Kieran?" I whispered back, reaching out for him, but paused. Jake, Levi and my mother were moving ever so slowly. My eyes widened as I gazed at Kieran.

"Why aren't you slowed like them?"

"I put a protection spell on myself that shields me against slowing or freezing spells," he said, the corner of his mouth twitching into a slight smile.

I stared at him. What a smart man. He was the only one that knew I could slow down time.

"Oh, Kieran." I closed the gap between us in seconds and fell into his embrace. His arms were strong around me as his lips brushed my hair and he nuzzled my head. The last of my strength severed. He held me up.

"Are you okay?"

"I feel so weak." I said.

He nodded, "too much magic."

"I was trapped." I blurted out, tears running down my face. "It was so horrible. I couldn't control anything I was doing."

"It's okay, you're safe now." His arms around me were so comforting.

"What have you done?" my mother bellowed.

Turning back to my mother, I jumped out of Kieran's arms. Kieran wrapped an arm around my waist, determined to keep me close to him or to keep me from falling. I didn't know which — probably both.

"It's not what I've done that matters," Kieran spat.

Levi pressed his back against the wall, and Jake, now standing, backed away — I didn't blame them. I could see the fury in my mother's eyes.

"It's over," Kieran said, standing his ground.

My mother laughed. "It's nowhere near over. Your city is mine now, boy."

A scream sounded off to the right, drawing our attention. Glancing back at my mother, I saw her heels running in the opposite direction. She had seized the moment and disappeared around the corner.

"Where is she?" Jake questioned as he turned back.

"Gone," I said bluntly.

Kieran released me, watching that I could hold myself up before trudging forward. He looked around the corner.

"Nowhere in sight."

WALKING THROUGH THE destruction was heartbreaking. The translucent ground was covered in shattered glass, reflecting the bright morning sun like a million tiny suns.

Deceased bodies were lying here and there. Everywhere we looked, we saw death and destruction, and despair that seemed to permeate the air. Kieran reached down toward the body lying on the ground near us.

"Kyra..." he whispered, placing a hand on the small woman's shoulder.

I wasn't sure if I had seen her before, but Kieran definitely knew her.

Kieran stood and a growl escape his lips, "Use your senses to find them."

Levi's eyes squinted, a deep crease forming on his forehead. Jake, Kieran, and I closed our eyes. Reaching out, I opened my mind and body, attuning to my surroundings. I could hear smashing glass in the distance. I searched, focusing on where the fight had moved to. My senses took me in and around the buildings until I could see someone hiding behind a wall. They were crouched down, clutching their abdomen, wincing in agony.

"I found Clara," I said, snapping my eyes open.

Kieran and Jake both abruptly opened their eyes and stared at me.

"Where?" Kieran asked.

"This way." I pointed toward the mansion.

We picked up the pace, diving in and around buildings to keep out of sight. We could hear yelling and more glass shattering; the sounds grew louder as we drew closer.

Something gripped my ankle, and I almost toppled over. Looking down, I saw a man with brown hair and grey eyes I recognised from the cave. His gaze fixed upon me, intense and unreadable. I shook my ankle to break free from his grip, but he held on with every last ounce of his strength.

"Trixie..."

"Let go of her," Kieran demanded, as he pulled me free.

"Trixie, please, listen," he croaked.

I stared down at the familiar man. Kieran still had hold of my waist protectively. Levi moved to my other side.

The man caught sight of Levi's face. "You made the right choice."

I glanced at Levi. He avoided my gaze, staring back at the Dark Soul Weaver.

"Trixie...only you can save..." he spluttered blood down his chin and I winced at the sight.

Taking a breath to steady myself, I knelt down beside him. His abdomen was soaked, the glistening of the blood barely discernible against the black.

"Save your...father." His eyes went blank as he released his last breath.

I reached down, closed his eyelids, and looked up at Levi and Kieran. "What does that mean?"

Kieran shook his head.

"I can't save someone who is—" I began.

"Being controlled," Levi finished, his expression blank.

"What?" I blinked.

Levi muttered, "I should have realised."

"Realised what?" I stood up, getting agitated.

"Your eyes were distant, glassy, when you were under the spell," he explained. "Just like his. I never noticed how glassy his eyes were until now."

Moving closer to the battle up ahead, we peered around the corner of a building. We watched my father from a distance; he was holding the shield in place. Soul Weavers were falling like flies being sprayed by insect repellent. The Dark Soul Weavers and Soul Hunters had no mercy.

"You're telling me...my father is being controlled, too?"

Levi nodded.

Fear clawed at my throat as anxiety gripped me. My knees buckled and my legs gave way. Kieran reached out and held onto me. Tension radiated from his muscles.

"I am her weakness," Kieran repeated to no one in particular.

I looked up at Kieran, my brow furrowed.

"You care for me, so I was the one who could free you

from your spell," he explained.

I shifted my eyes to Levi. He looked away, expressionless.

Kieran continued, "If your father still cares for you, *you* will be his weakness."

I thought about that for a moment while watching my father intently. He held a strong posture, his shoulders squared and both his hands out in front of him, holding the magic shield up.

"What if he's not being controlled? Or what if he doesn't care about me anymore?"

"What if he does?" Levi said.

I stared into Levi's eyes for a long moment. I could sense there was more to his words than he was letting on.

"You can save him," Kieran stated.

I shook my head. "What if I can't? What if he doesn't—?"

"You were still in there and cared enough to save me." Kieran looked deep into my eyes. "He could still be in there, too."

My stomach twisted. My breathing was uneven as I stared back into Kieran's mesmerising eyes.

As though feeling my tension, Kieran rubbed my arms and said, "You can do this."

I released a breath and nodded. "So, what's the plan?"

"I will go to Clara," Jake stated.

Kieran inclined his head to Jake before turning back to me.

"You need to get his attention by putting yourself in danger," Kieran announced reluctantly. "If you're in danger, he will save you. If he saves you, you in return save him."

Twenty-Six

TRIXIE

A SOUL WEAVER FLEW THROUGH the air past us. The woman hit her head on a glass wall and fell to the ground, unconscious. I remembered her from the portal room — Mae. I fought the urge to go to her aid. The rise and fall of her chest comforted me, if only a little.

"Let's remember our main mission," Kieran stated, glancing sideways at Mae.

Levi and I nodded in unison.

"Save my father," I said, "then we might have a

chance against my mother."

Kieran shifted awkwardly. "Let's go."

Making our way down the path, we found where the primary fight was taking place—right in front of the mansion entrance. There were Soul Weavers congregated around the edges of the buildings. Demetri was fighting someone on the stairs. All the Soul Hunters and most of the Dark Soul Weavers were behind my father's massive orange shield. Delaras was standing beside my father; my mother was nowhere to be seen.

The amber shield had a magnificent beauty about it. My father was standing in the centre of the force field; his focus was on keeping the shield active. Spells were flying back and forth between the parties. The area was filled with colour—it would be a stunningly beautiful sight if not for the situation.

"Ok, get the attention of a Dark Soul Weaver," Kieran said. "Make sure you stay in your father's field of vision. Once you have their attention, only cast defensively."

Fidgeting with my fingers, I stared at the fireballs flying back and forth across the city, my heart pounding in my ears.

"I...I don't know if..."

"You can do this," Kieran reassured me. "We will be right behind you."

I gazed up into his eyes, his face expressionless, but his jaw was tense. Something about him was off. I opened my mouth to speak, but thought better of it and closed it again. I nodded and stepped forward.

Kieran's hand caught my arm and spun me around to face him. His tongue flicked against the corner of my lip and he pressed his lips to mine. I arched myself toward him, leaning into his chest and wrapping my hands around his neck.

I wanted to stay like this forever, but I knew we couldn't, and we had company. *Shit, Levi.* Reluctantly, but hastily, I broke the embrace and stepped back. I avoided Levi's gaze, but I could feel the burn of his eyes on me.

"Alright, let's do this." I said, and I stepped forward, leaving Kieran and Levi standing together awkwardly.

I snuck toward the chaos and ducked behind a tree. Peering around it, I searched the area for the perfect place to move to. There was a line of trees along this side of the building; I carefully ran from tree to tree to move closer. Now, standing within my father's peripheral vision, I was in the prime position.

I glanced back and saw Kieran and Levi following me behind the row of trees. Kieran nodded to me encouragingly. I took a breath and stepped out into the open.

Casting a spell at the nearest Dark Soul Weaver, I quickly got his attention. His shoulder length steel blue hair was vibrant compared to the dark clothing he wore. He stepped toward me, throwing a dark forest-green fireball back at me. *That's it; attack me.* Jumping aside, his spell hit the tree instead.

I threw a ball of electricity at him; it hit him on the shoulder and burnt a hole in his shirt. *Only cast defensively,* Kieran's voice rang in my ears. *Oops.* The man growled as he conjured up a large ball of swirling magic. My eyes widened as he released it toward me.

A small orange ball appeared in front of me and expanded as it surrounded me. I stared at the amber swirls, confused and surprised. It flabbergasted the Dark Soul Weaver, and his shot hit the shield and dissipated.

Orange. I looked over at my father. His massive shield protecting all the other Dark Soul Weavers and Soul Hunters had collapsed. He was walking through the scampering crowd, and another spell erupted from his hands. As the Dark Soul Weaver turned, my father's spell hit him in the face. The man was knocked off his feet.

I smiled at my father. "Dad?"

He bounded over to me, and the surrounding shield vanished as he gripped me into a tight hug.

"Oh, Trixie pixie, I'm so sorry." He said.

Trixie Pixie. My childhood nickname he gave me. I wrapped my arms around my father; it felt so surreal to have him back.

"No, Dad, I'm sorry. I wish I had known. I could have saved you so long ago," I said.

He shook his head, stepping back. "No, don't be sorry. You weren't to know."

Kieran and Levi appeared at my side. My father stared at Levi. A fireball flew past us as the pandemonium behind us continued.

"Don't worry. Levi is on our side," I reassured him.

My father nodded, then turned his eyes on Kieran.

"Dad, this —."

"Kieran." My father's voice cracked.

I blinked. *My father knew him?* Looking back and forth between my father and my boyfriend, I frowned. My father's lips parted and his head bobbed. His eyes welled up with tears and spilled over his cheeks. My eyes widened. Kieran stared at him, expressionless.

"I—I'm so sorry." He said through the tears.

I didn't have a clue what was going on, but they must have known each other personally somehow.

Kieran swallowed. "It wasn't you."

"But I-I did it," my father replied, his voice breaking again.

"Yes, but it wasn't the real you, as we discovered about half an hour ago." Kieran shook his head.

"Does someone want to tell me—" I began, but a loud shriek pierced our ears.

"NO!"

We turned to see my mother standing only metres away.

"You take my daughter, now my husband!" She yelled.

My father threw his hands up and immediately conjured another shield to protect all four of us. My mother didn't even flinch from the sudden shield appearing.

"You took my free-will," my father yelled as he threw a spell at my mother. "Then you took my daughter's free-will."

"*Our* daughter," my mother spat as she evaded his spell.

"I'm *not* your daughter," I barked. "You lost your daughter the day you left."

My mother stared at me, furious. "You wouldn't understand. You were just a child."

"And this doesn't make it right!" my father yelled.

A knot of anxious confusion twisted in my gut, making me feel sick. My eyes darted back and forth between the two speakers. *What were they talking about?*

"My son would still be alive if it wasn't for *that* one's parents," she screamed, jerking her head toward Kieran.

Kieran frowned. I glanced at him; he clearly didn't know what she was referring to either. *My parents had a son? I had a brother?* An avalanche of emotions surged within me, but I was too overwhelmed to process them.

"He was in the wrong place at the wrong time," my father shot back.

"Of course you would say that; he wasn't *your* son."

What? My head whirled. *Not his son?* I was missing vital pieces of these conversations and I couldn't keep up. My head whirled like a cyclone.

"I still cared for him, loved him like he was my own," he said. "Doing what you're doing won't bring him back."

"No, it won't." She said. "But I will get my revenge

instead. I will grow in power and take over the Soul Weavers!"

I glanced around at the others fighting nearby. So many glassy eyes. My jaw dropped and my eyes widened.

"They're *all* under your control? None of them are themselves?" I questioned in horror.

My mother smiled wickedly. "She's worked it out."

"You're taking control over everyone, so you hold the power. That way, nothing else can be taken from you," I mumbled.

"Very good." My mother nodded her approval.

We all looked over toward the battle. Some were clutching their bodies in pain, some were lying on the ground unconscious. Others were still fighting, but getting exhausted.

"It's time you stop this," Kieran said, bringing our attention back to my mother.

"Can't you see?" She smirked, opening her arms wide and gesturing around her. "You are losing."

"No," my father began, "you are."

His hand flew up in front of him. Before anyone could react, a spell hit my mother in the chest, and she collapsed.

"Quick, she won't stay down for long." My father moved toward the crowd as his shield dropped from around us. We followed without hesitation.

"Stand with me!" my father bellowed.

The battle didn't stop. Fireballs continued flying

across the area, casting a colourful glow on the faces of everyone in front of them.

"Let's take Myrdreya back!" Kieran yelled out.

Jake and Clara came around a corner and stood beside Kieran. Kieran looked over at Clara.

"Alright?" He said.

She gave him a quick nod. "I'm fine."

My father conjured another shield to protect us. Dark Soul Weavers and Soul Hunters glanced at one another, confusion stricken across their faces. They were not the ones being shielded anymore. A few other Soul Weavers joined us behind the shield; others were hesitant.

"He's on our side. He was being controlled." Kieran shouted to the ambivalent Soul Weavers.

The colourful sparks from the flying fireballs continued as, one by one, the Soul Weavers stepped with us.

"You were too quick to trust he's actually on our side." Demetri's sullen voice came from behind us.

"And you're being too quick to deny the protection of his shield." Kieran spat back.

The remaining Soul Weavers moved to stand behind the amber shield. The Dark Soul Weavers ceased fire, and the Soul Hunters stepped back a few paces.

"Surrender or leave," Demetri yelled, his hand ready.

The Dark Soul Weavers and Soul Hunters stared in disbelief. Mortified, they looked at each other for a moment and then turned to run past my mother, who was picking herself up from the ground.

"No! What have you done?" she screamed as her followers dashed past her and didn't look back.

"Go with them and never come back," Demetri spat at her.

"What? You're letting her go?" Kieran stepped toward Demetri.

Demetri hesitated before he spoke. "She is no threat to us now."

"How would we know that?"

"She's lost everything that gave her leverage. She's done." Demetri eyed Julianne.

My mother stared at us. We stood together, protected by my father's shield. Her eyes darted between us and landed on me. She let out an ear-piercing scream before turning and racing away. We followed them to the portal room to ensure they had taken a portal out of the city. Once gone, my father brought down his shield.

Twenty-Seven

"SO, WE HAVE A SOUL Hunter and a Dark Soul Weaver on our side," Demetri stated, his emerald eyes dark.

I grinned, "Not a dark one anymore, and not a hunter anymore."

"Please accept our apology for we were being controlled by Julianne," my father announced.

Levi hadn't been controlled, but I wasn't about to correct him.

Demetri stared for a moment. "Julianne was always a

master of controlling minds."

I glanced at my father. He placed a comforting arm around my shoulders.

Kieran stepped forward and said, "Levi gave me the information to save Trixie from being controlled. I could save her because I cared for her, and she cared for me. We saved her father the same way because he still cared for Trixie."

Demetri looked at the faces in the crowd. His jaw was clenched; his eyes distant. Everyone stared at him expectantly.

Demetri eyed us for a few moments before saying, "Take them to the cells."

Soul Weavers grabbed Levi, my father, and I by the arms — one on each side. *Dungeons?* I did not know there were dungeons on the glass island; Kieran had never mentioned it.

"Kieran?" I reached for him, pushing against the guards holding me.

Kieran reached out for me but another Soul Weaver grabbed his arm and wrenched him back to Demetri, twisted his arm behind his back. The men holding Levi, my father and I paused and listened.

"You can't be serious?" Kieran blundered at Demetri.

Demetri glared at him. "Do I look like I'm kidding?"

"She helped us take back Myrdreya. She was being controlled!"

"She also let *them* in," Demetri spat, his lip curling.

"Take him to the dungeons, too."

"What?" Kieran struggled as another Soul Weaver gripped him.

"Just let me explain, please," I begged.

Demetri waved a hand to indicate to take us away, ignoring my plea entirely.

"Let's get this city back in order." I heard Demetri's voice behind us.

The guards took us through the city, gripping our arms. We entered a building nearby Demetri's tower. Two guards stood on either side of a locked gate; a thick glass gate. *How hadn't I seen this before?*

The guards unlocked the gate for us to pass through. I was the last to be ushered through; I glanced behind me as the gate closed and locked. A flash of light faintly peered through the glass; I frowned, narrowing my eyes.

"That's right. Don't get any ideas of trying to escape," the Soul Weaver at my right arm said. "Touch that gate, and you will be knocked unconscious. And it won't be pleasant either."

My eyes widened slightly as the gate went out of sight. I looked forward again.

We were led down a spiralling staircase, down into the depths of the glass island—or below it. We walked along a short corridor before the men who held us stopped. Levi, my father, and I were thrown into one cell, and Kieran was thrown into another opposite us. The guards retreated from the corridor and were out of sight.

There were no windows; even if there were, we would only see clouds, anyway. My father sat down in a corner, making himself comfortable—or as comfortable as he could be. I stood by the cell door, looking around the glass cell.

"Can't we just use magic to get out?" Levi asked Kieran.

"Do you think they would bother putting us in cells if we could get out of them?" Kieran asked bitterly.

I glanced over at Levi, frowning. He avoided my gaze, knowing how stupid he must have sounded.

"These cells are re-enforced with magic, stopping magic users from using magic within the cell," Kieran explained. "And don't bother trying to break the glass. It's too strong."

I looked around the cell. The glass floor and walls were so thick that I couldn't determine how far inside the glass island we were. The cell doors were like a prison; rounded bars, but made of glass. The glass wasn't very thick. In fact, they looked like they could easily break if kicked with enough force. They must be much more durable than they appeared to be.

I leant against the cell wall. My father was seated in the corner to my right, with his head against the back wall. Levi stood opposite me; he didn't seem to know what to do.

"So, can you tell me what you two were talking about earlier?" I asked, looking from Kieran to my father.

"Which part?" My father sighed. "Your mother and I murdered Kieran's parents. We went to his home and...attacked."

My mouth dropped open. The images that filled my mind made me ill.

"Correction," Kieran chimed in, "*she* killed my parents; you were under a spell and had no control of your actions."

"You knew all this time that I was the daughter of your parents' murderer?" I whispered across the dungeon to Kieran.

Kieran adverted his eyes; I couldn't read his expression. Kieran had forgiven my father so easily; he had such a good heart. I took a deep breath and released it. I stared at the ground just as I heard footsteps.

I looked across at Kieran; he was staring down the corridor toward the sound of boots on glass. I moved across the space of the cell and peered out as a Soul Weaver came into view.

"Jake," Kieran breathed, "I'm glad to see you."

Jake nodded at Kieran and then eyed the three of us in the opposite cell.

"I've come to take you to speak with Demetri," Jake announced, his voice was blunt.

Kieran lifted his chin. "And what of the others?"

"You will all undergo questioning separately," Jake answered as he unlocked Kieran's cell.

Kieran stepped around Jake, over to me; he reached

for me through the cell bars. His hand softly touched my cheek as I cupped my hand over his.

"It will be okay," he whispered.

"Come, he doesn't like to wait," Jake said thickly, an unusual demeanour coming from him.

Looking over at Jake, I saw someone else standing by the stairs behind him. *Was that the cause of his bluntness?* I hadn't heard him speak like this before, especially not to Kieran. I gave Kieran a weak smile and nodded to reassure him I was okay.

I watched as they went out of sight. Leaning back against the wall, I ground my teeth and pulled at my fingers as we waited. Levi tapped against the glass behind him. My father sat in silence.

After a while, Jake returned. I looked behind him, but Kieran wasn't with him.

"Kieran?" I asked.

"I'm sorry, Trixie. I am not allowed to disclose the Soul Council's decisions," he said before unlocking the cell door. "Levi, your turn."

I swallowed. *What did that mean? Was he let off? Had he been...* I didn't want to think about the worst-case scenario.

Levi glanced over at me. I nodded at him. He left the cell, and Jake immediately locked the door again. Another half-hour went by and my fingers were becoming raw.

"Are you okay?" My father's voice broke the silence.

"I don't know; are you?" I replied, my voice shaking.

He nodded. "Yes, I will be."

I pushed myself off the wall and lowered myself down beside him. It felt strange to have my father back after so many years.

"I'm sorry for what you had to go through." His voice cracked.

"Dad..."

"Please, just listen," he said. "I never thought I would have control back again. I thought she had taken it from me forever. I thought you were gone forever."

I bit my lip and stared at my feet.

"One thing she never took from me is how much I love you," he continued. "She could control my body, but she could not control my real thoughts."

I sniffed, tears dripping down my cheeks. *When had I started crying?*

"I love you, Trixie. I never stopped."

Opening my mouth, I let out a small cry as tears pooled in my eyes. I sniffed again as I turned to him. He reached and wiped away my tears.

"It's going to be okay," he reassured me with a small smile. "You're safe now."

Out of the corner of my eye, I saw a figure standing at our cell door. I looked up and saw Jake watching us. His expression was thoughtful and pained. I wiped away the tears. Jake stared at me for a moment before recovering himself and unlocking the door.

"Jay," he said.

My father stood up and walked toward the cell door. I pushed myself off the floor.

"Dad, wait," I said.

He turned around and looked at me.

I dashed across the cell and crashed myself against his chest. "I love you, too."

He gripped me tightly, holding me against him. I didn't want to let him go. I was afraid that I would never see him again. My body trembled with terror.

"Sorry to break this reunion, but..." Jake said.

We broke apart. I nodded to Jake and stepped back. My father left the cell, and Jake locked it again. Jake nodded quickly to me before grabbing my father by the arm and leading him away.

Alone again. I slumped against the back wall, staring at nothing in particular. Everything was crumbling around me. My chest tightened as I brought my knees up to it. Wrapping my arms around my knees, hugging myself, I rocked back and forth.

Tears rolled down my face as I stared at the space in front of me. My body trembled uncontrollably. I was frightened and sombre. *Will I ever see Kieran again? We are all innocent. Surely, they know that? What if they had eliminated him?*

I hyperventilated. Swallowing around a lump in my throat, I continued to rock backwards and forwards. I stared straight ahead at the glass bars.

Doubling over, I closed my eyes. Shaking my head

vigorously, I tried to escape the thoughts that pained me. I felt like I was being crushed again. As if the ocean was swallowing me whole.

"Trixie?"

I lifted my head. Jake was standing outside the cell, staring wide-eyed at the glass surrounding me. My eyes mimicked his as I stared at the sight before us.

Every part of the room I sat in was warped. The floor was not flat, but wavy instead. The walls were leaning in towards me as if they threatened to crush me. The cell bars were tangled and twisted with each other.

"Jake...can you see that?" I asked hesitantly.

He nodded, still staring.

I squeezed my eyes shut for a moment. When I reopened them, the walls returned to their original state. The bars untwisted and morphed back into their solid vertical form.

Jake's jaw had dropped as he watched everything move back into place.

"How...?" He couldn't finish his question as he stared at me.

I shook my head. "I-I don't know. Please, don't tell anyone."

"Does Kieran know?" he asked.

I shook my head again, my eyes pleading. He glanced sideways down the hall before unlocking the cell door and walking in. I pushed myself up from the floor, keeping my back to the wall.

"How long have you been able to do that?" He eyed me suspiciously.

"Since I can remember," I replied. "But I have no control over it. It happens when…"

He raised his eyebrows, waiting for me to continue.

I took a breath and released it in a big whoosh.

"It happens when I'm upset or extremely anxious," I slowly answered. "Please, Jake, tell no one."

He nodded slowly but said nothing.

"It's your turn," he said, composing himself and stepping to the side, allowing me to pass.

Taking another breath, I passed him and exited the cell. He followed me, not holding onto my arm like he had with Levi and my father. I wasn't sure if it was because he was afraid to touch me, or if he just trusted me. I hoped it was the latter.

We walked in silence up the spiralling staircase we had descended earlier. When we reached the locked gate, Jake spoke to the guards quickly. They removed the spell and unlocked the gate. Jake walked through first, indicating to me to follow. The guards eyed me warily, noting that Jake wasn't holding onto me.

Jake veered left toward a door I didn't notice hours before. He pushed the door open and tilted his head toward it. I swallowed and stepped through the doorway into another room.

Demetri and the other Soul Council members were sitting at a table, waiting. The door closed with a thud behind me. I turned around to see Jake standing by the door with his hands behind his back.

"Trixie, take a seat," Demetri stated.

I turned back to the door. There was only one way in and one way out. Thick glass walls and no windows. My heart raced as I felt all eyes on me. There was a lonesome chair in the middle facing the council. Walking over to the chair, I seated myself and looked at the faces staring at me.

"You are being questioned today because we found you fighting with our enemy," Demetri stated. "How long have you known about this invasion?"

I swallowed, my palms sweating under my fingertips.

"I didn't know." I said.

Demetri narrowed his eyes and said, "Didn't know what exactly? That they were planning it?"

I frowned. "No, of course not."

"Did you take the mission of distracting Julianne and Jay's army away from Myrdreya so that you could escape?"

"What? No, I..."

"When you went to the forest and disappeared, you claim you were taken. Is that correct?" Demetri's voice was monotone.

"Yes, they chased us and..."

"Chased us? Who is *us*?" Demetri asked, interrupting me once again.

"Kieran," I replied. "They..."

Demetri continued to interrupt me. "Did Kieran help you get back to your parents?"

I ground my teeth. "No, *they* took *me!*"

"Took you? How?"

"They chased us and pushed Kieran through his portal and knocked me out. I woke up in an underground cave somewhere."

Demetri's expression didn't change. His emerald eyes burned into my soul. *Where was Kieran?* Surely he told the Soul Council this already. My breathing was rapid and my heartbeat thumped in my chest.

"Do you know where this cave is?" he queried.

I shook my head. "No, I wasn't allowed to leave, so I never saw sunlight until I opened a portal into Myrdreya."

"Ah-ha! So you admit that you opened a portal for the Dark Soul Weavers and Soul Hunters to enter our city?"

"Yes, but not on purpose." I shifted in the chair uncomfortably.

"Do you admit that when you brought them into Myrdreya, you fought against us?" Demetri asked sternly.

"I was forced!" I blurted out, my bottled up anger erupting.

Demetri raised his eyebrows.

"She had a spell on me. I had no control over my actions," I said, the corners of my eyes wet. "I was screaming at myself to stop, but my body wouldn't listen."

A tear dripped from my right eye, and when no one said anything, I continued.

"I was her puppet. I could do nothing but follow her instructions. When my mother tried to attack Kieran, I snapped out of the spell."

I gazed over their staring faces.

"How did you snap out of it?" Demetri asked.

"Levi explained to Kieran that he was my weakness. His..." It was never how much he cared, it dawned on me. "...his love for me broke the spell. The same way I saved my father from the spell; I was his weakness."

A smile played at the corner of Demetri's mouth.

"Please, you have to believe me. I would never hurt a Soul Weaver on purpose. She forced both my father and me," I pleaded, my heart racing a million miles an hour.

After a very long, agonising, silent minute, he announced, "You are exempt from your crimes."

"What?" *All that hounding — had they known the truth all along? Did they just want to torture me?*

"Thank you for helping us save our city, Trixie," Demetri stated.

I blinked. "Where is Kieran? My father? Levi? Where are they?"

He waved a hand. "Don't worry, they are all fine. I'm sorry we had interrogated you. We had to be sure."

I glared at Demetri, but kept my mouth shut.

"You are free to leave. Jake will escort you to the others." Demetri stood up from the long table, indicating to Jake—who was still standing by the door.

I looked over at Jake. He opened the door and nodded to me. I quickly stood and hurried across to him, determined to escape the enclosed room.

"Trixie, one more thing," Demetri added.

Swallowing a lump in my throat, I paused by the door and looked over my shoulder.

"Use your gift wisely. Learn to control it."

My heart skipped a beat. Panic arose. *He couldn't be referring to the room warping, could he?*

Jake must have sensed my tension, as it was he who spoke. "I will ensure she learns to control her slowing ability."

I glanced at him, studying his expression for a moment. I let out a breath. They were talking about my ability to slow—a form of stasis—as Kieran had called it.

꙳ ● ꙳

JAKE OPENED A door in the mansion—a door down a corridor I hadn't been before. An instant wave of relief washed over my body as three familiar faces stared back at me. Kieran stood straight away at the sight of me. A few quick strides and I collapsed into his arms. All my anxiety dissolved as he held me tightly against his chest.

Glancing at my father, I could see a small smile as he stared at me. I couldn't imagine my life with him; now, I couldn't imagine my life without him. I grinned back at him. My attention drew to Levi, who was watching me from a lounge chair on the other side of the room. He smiled at me—I could see straight through it, though.

Wriggling myself out of Kieran's embrace, I crossed the room to Levi. I sat down beside him; I could feel Kieran's eyes on me. Throwing my arms around Levi's shoulders, I hugged him tightly. His arms came up loosely around me. A touch I used to long for was now very foreign.

Twenty-Eight

KIERAN

S TANDING AWKWARDLY BESIDE TRIXIE OUTSIDE the portal room, I watched how fluently she and Levi moved together. After all that happened over the last 6 months, and despite all that happened between them, I was concerned she would choose him.

He betrayed her.

He left her alone.

Would she go back to him?

Those thoughts were circling around in my head as I

watched. The sinking ship in my heart sunk again—and she wasn't on it.

"Do you have to go?" Trixie said to him, a hand gently touching his forearm.

"I don't belong here," Levi replied, his hand lightly covering hers.

If she chose him, I would not be around when she did.

I snuck away. Walking down the path toward the garden, I momentarily glanced back.

Why did I look back?

Trixie kissed Levi on the cheek. I raced around the corner, distancing myself from them as soon as I could.

No matter how much I tried to deny it, I couldn't erase the sinking feeling in the pit of my stomach. She was going to choose him.

Twenty-Nine

"I WILL ASK DEMETRI FOR permission to allow you to stay," I said. "You assisted us in saving Myrdreya."

Levi glanced away for a moment. "Thank you, but I don't belong here. I'm not magical, and this is an opportunity for me to go live a normal life."

Averting my eyes, I realised Kieran had disappeared. I glanced around for a moment before bringing my attention back to Levi.

"It's time we move on," Levi said, holding my hand.

"We need to put this chapter behind us and learn from our mistakes."

Knowing Levi was right, I leant in and kissed him on the cheek. After all, I couldn't truly move on with my new life if he was around. The memories would continue to haunt me.

"Thank you for saving me. If it wasn't for you, Kieran wouldn't have known how to save me." I smiled.

He returned the smile, but it was sad. "He is good for you. He loves you, you know?"

My lips parted as I considered his words. Love was always a strong word to me; I never used it lightly. Words I was afraid of hearing. I didn't know if I could say them back. I loved Levi for so long that I had been so scared of loving someone else.

"Goodbye, Trixie." Levi tightly hugged me.

A portal was swirling behind us, ready to take him home. He released me and stepped around me. I heard the intake of his breath as he stepped through. And, just like that, he was gone again.

I stared at the portal as it swirled and vanished. I didn't know whether I would ever see him again, but I knew he was right—it was time to move on.

Leaving the portal room, I trudged down the pathway leading toward the gardens. I had a feeling I would find Kieran there; I was sure it was his favourite place in Myrdreya—as it was mine.

As I walked through Myrdreya, the last of the broken

glass was being magically repaired. Soul Weavers were scattered throughout the city, using their abilities to repair it.

Turning the corner into the garden, I saw his beautiful brown hair worse for wear. His normally neat spiked hair was sticking up at odd angles. His back was turned to me and he was seated, unmoving, on the garden chair.

I slowly approached him. My heart was jumping out of my ribs; I didn't know what I was going to say. I wiped my sweaty palms on the sides of my jeans.

I took a deep breath. "Kieran?"

He spun around to face me. He looked surprised to see me. My heart pounded; he was as beautiful as the first day I met him—when he saved my life.

"Trixie, I wasn't sure you would come."

The rogue strand of hair still rested on his forehead. I smiled to myself and sat beside him.

"I knew I would find you here." I said.

He shifted awkwardly, his hands clenched together in front of his body. He seemed so distant, his mouth a pinched line. His eyes darted around the garden, anywhere and everywhere except for looking at me. The surrounding air was thick with a heavy emotion; an emotion I couldn't read. I could feel my heart pounding, my thoughts racing, and my palms sweating.

"I understand if you are leaving..." He said.

My heart threatened to leap right out of my chest.

"Leaving?" my brows pulled together. "Why would

you think I'm leaving?"

"Levi isn't staying…" His voice trailed off.

Why was he talking about Levi?

I looked at him, confused. "No, he's not. He's going to go find a normal life."

His beautiful eyes finally met mine. "You mean, you're staying?"

"Of course, I…" I reached out and placed my hand on his thigh. "I wanted to stay with you."

His expression changed. His uncertainty washed away.

"I thought…" he licked his lips and took a breath. "I thought you had chosen him."

"What?" I shook my head. "No, I—I have a history with him, but that's all it is. I want to be with you."

The tension in his shoulders melted as he turned to face me. He reached for my hands and laced his fingers in mine. He released a faint sigh and smiled.

"I want to be with you, too." His lips twitched.

I sighed, smiling at his beautiful face.

"I love you, Trixie."

I fell forward and planted my lips on his. Throwing my arms around him, his hands sat softly on my waist. I was surprised at myself when I realised all I wanted to do was say those three words back to him.

Pulling away, but staying close to his face, I said, "I love you, too."

He pressed his lips hard on mine. There, I said it, and

it felt right. It was like a weight had lifted from my shoulders as soon as the words rolled off my tongue. I was finally at peace. The ocean that had been crushing my soul has finally dissolved into oxygen. I could breathe again. And I had Kieran to thank for resurrecting my soul.

Shattered SOULS

SOUL WEAVER SEQUEL

CHANTELLE LAMBERT

One

STARING OUT MY RAIN-STRICKEN bedroom window in the darkness, all I could hear was my parents arguing downstairs. It wasn't unusual. It occurred every week, and every week it was the same argument. Me. There's a glass city called Myrdreya; a city my mother wanted to move us to. She told me the city was a safe-zone for people like us—Soul Weavers. My father didn't want to move. He believed we were in no danger and wanted us to live a relatively normal life with the non-magic humans.

"We're not normal!" My mother's frustrated voice trailed up the stairs.

"Doesn't mean we can't try to be." My father's voice followed.

"Our son needs the training they can provide."

Little did they know I had been training on my own for months now. Dazed, I watched the droplets cry on my window. Even the rain couldn't drown out their yelling. I outstretched my hand, flexing my fingers. Purple swirls of electricity sparked from my fingertips. The magic grew as it engulfed my hand; a ball of energy rotated in my palm. My eyes were locked on it, mesmerised by my own power.

Out of the corner of my eye, in the pouring rain, something bright caught my attention. Releasing the energy back into my body, I dropped to the floor and peered out the window. By the enormous tree in our backyard, a swirling silver portal had appeared. My parents had told me about portals, but I had never seen one before – until now.

I stared as a man stepped out of the portal. His sleek black hair hung around his shoulders, a long black trench coat trailed behind him as he walked forward. The portal faded and disappeared behind him. He moved as though the rain didn't even bother him. Whoever this man was, he didn't look friendly. Careful to keep low to the ground, I scurried across my bedroom and quietly opened my door.

My parents' arguing reached my ears again as I hurried down the stairs. I leapt off the second-last stair and ran into the kitchen where their voices were coming from.

"There's a Soul Weaver in our backyard." I said.

They stopped mid-sentence and stared at me.

"Get down." My father whispered, pushing my mother toward me.

We bent down and huddled behind the kitchen bench. None of us were combat trained; if this Soul Weaver was here to hurt us, we wouldn't stand a chance. Panic arose in my chest. My heart thumped behind my ribs as my mother held onto my arm.

"Mum, we have to get out of here."

She put a finger to her lips to shush me.

"Mum, please, I don't think —."

A blast came from the back of the house, drowning out my words. I looked up to see my father sprawled on the floor. He rolled over, pushing himself back to his feet.

"Lucas, why?" I heard my father say.

Lucas? Why would my father's friend attack us? My eyebrows pulled together as I watched my father defend himself from another spell.

"Because we can't live amongst humans. We don't belong with them. And you..." Lucas spat, "you want to live in peace with them?"

"There's nothing wrong with living with the humans, they know nothing about us," my father said as he took a careful step forward.

A burst of wind with a silver energy ball flew past the bench and hit my father in the chest. Blasted off his feet, he immediately went out of our line of sight.

"Dad!" I stood and yelled.

Oops. There goes our hiding place. My mother tugged on the hem of my pants, I discreetly gestured to her with my hand to stay down. Lucas glared at me.

"Ah, Kieran. Is your mother here too?" he glanced around the room.

I shook my head. "No, she's working late tonight."

He stared at me silently, and I wondered if he had called my bluff. My mother let go of my clothing and I stepped forward to get out of her reach. The last thing I wanted was her to be in danger too.

"Stop right there." Lucas growled.

I paused and glanced at my father's body lying on the floor, unmoving.

"He's fine, just knocked out." Lucas folded his arms across his chest. "So, Kieran, tell me, how much magic training have you had?"

"I know enough." I eyed him suspiciously; strange question to ask.

His mouth twisted into a smirk, "in other words, no formal training. Did your parents keep you from learning the ways of Soul Weavers?"

I shifted on my feet, forcing myself to not turn to look at my mother. Swallowing, I ground my teeth as I thought over his words. My mother wanted me to go to Myrdreya, to not only be safe but to train. My father had other plans.

"Come with me, and I will teach you everything I know." Lucas said, stepping toward me. "You're what.. .sixteen?"

"Fifteen." I corrected.

He nodded, "right, close enough. Join me, Kieran, and I will teach you everything your parents never did."

My heartbeat thumped in my ears. My chest tightened as I glanced from my father to Lucas. I didn't dare glance at my mother.

"I'm fine, thank you. I can learn on my own."

"Very well..." Lucas's voice changed. "You leave me no choice then..."

My mother didn't allow him to finish. She jumped out of her hiding place and threw her hand out in front of her. A royal-blue energy ball instantly left her palm and stopped in front of me. It grew larger, filling the space in between Lucas and I, shielding me from him.

I took a step back. The shield followed me like a magnet. Another royal-blue ball flew past me; this time it hit Lucas square in the face.

"You lying little — ."

He didn't get his words out. Another ball hit him; this time it was bright-green. I turned to find my father standing with his feet apart and a hand outstretched in front. His expression was determined.

"HOW DARE YOU!" my father boomed.

Lucas's eyes dashed from me to my mother and father before he turned and bolted away. Three against one—the odds were not in his favour. My father bounded through the kitchen after him. I swiftly followed him out into the backyard. We stood side by side staring at the space before us; Lucas was gone.

WITH NO SIGN of Lucas for two weeks, my father deemed us safe again. My mother wasn't convinced, and neither was I.

I was constantly feeling like we were being watched. *What were they waiting for?*

My mother had secretly started training me, without my father knowing. He didn't want us to bring attention to our magic while living with the humans—*but what was the point in being a Soul Weaver then?*

A purple ball of energy shot out of my hand and hit the back door window, shattering it. I cast a quick glance at my mother, who was instantly casting a spell, her focus on the door. The shattered pieces of glass lifted from the ground and reformed together again as if it hadn't happened.

"Amazing. Imagine if we could just fix things for regular humans like that?" I joked.

"Then the world would be a more peaceful place." She said.

I stared at the sadness in her eyes for a moment.

"Why didn't we just portal to Myrdreya?" I asked my mother while my father was at the shop.

"You can't just portal into Myrdreya uninvited, you have to be escorted there. The shield around the city will throw us off the edge of the island the moment we portal in." She replied. "While your father is..."

"Stubborn?"

"Yes, stubborn...it's unlikely we will get there."

I frowned. "Where is Myrdreya exactly?"

"It's high in the sky." She smiled.

"An island in the sky?" I raised my eyebrows.

She nodded, her eyes glazing over as she looked off into the distance. "The most beautiful city you would ever see. Everything made from glass. The sun gleams off the surface like crystals."

I imagined a floating island high in the sky, made of solid glass, and grinned. A key turned in the lock on the front door, wiping the grin from my face. My father walked in a moment later. My mother grabbed the dishcloth and pretended she had just finished cleaning the kitchen.

"Hey, dad." I greeted.

He raises his eyebrows, "odd to see you down here."

"I was just getting a drink." I lied. *Nice to see you, too.*

I followed his eyes to my mother, who had just rinsed the cloth and hung it on the tap.

She turned and smiled over at him, "honey, did you

remember the milk?"

"Of course," he nodded as he stepped forward and placed the bag of groceries on the kitchen bench.

I slipped away upstairs, back to my bedroom before my father could ask me anything else. I closed my bedroom door to shut out their chatter; I wanted to avoid being around when they argued again.

Stunning colours of the sunset shone through my window. It was like the sky was on fire. The particles in the atmosphere were changing the directions of the light rays beautifully this afternoon. Somehow the phenomenon was so calming; I flopped down on my bed and allowed my worries to float away with the light.

EYES OPENING WITH a snap, I quickly realised it wasn't my eyes snapping—it was something else downstairs. I quietly climbed out of bed and froze. A loud bang sounded through the walls and floor. The blood left my face, dread washing over me.

Bolting for my bedroom door, I pulled it open and dashed down the hallway toward my parent's bedroom. I didn't quite make it to their room when my father stepped out. He grabbed my arm and pulled me into the room behind him, closing the door quietly.

"We should have left when we had the chance." I heard my mother whisper.

I searched the room for her; I hadn't been in my parent's room for what felt like years. It still looked the same; dark wooden king-size bed with a blue-patterned bedspread. Matching bedside tables sat on either side, topped with a black lamp. My mother crouched beside the bed, near the beside table.

My father ignored her comment and turned to me, "let's portal out of here before—."

The bedroom door blasted inward, smashing my father in the back. I jumped backwards as the sound of my mother's cry erupted around the room. My father fell forward, slamming to the ground with the door.

With his blue eyes and a goatee that matched his short trimmed black hair, I stared in horror at the man standing before us. My eyes widened as I stretched my hand out in front and cast a shield spell in the doorway, shielding us from the man. I glanced over to my mother; it was thanks to her that I knew how. Her eyes were locked on my father's; he reached a hand toward her.

"You know what to do," he hushed to her.

She nodded and looked directly at me. I stared at the man in the doorway; he thrust his hand against the shield. My father reached his hand forward and thrust a shield up in the doorway, his mahogany magic replacing my violet, just in time when my shield collapsed.

"Kieran, come," my mother pulled herself up, holding her hand out toward me.

We couldn't possibly be leaving without my father, could

we? I lifted the door off my father, pushing it to the side. He shook his head.

"No, leave me." He muttered.

A blast of orange light hit my shield—I stared wide-eyed at the man trying to break through. Reluctantly, I ran over to the mother, leaving my father on the floor, blood dripping from his head.

A portal appeared in the ensuite behind me, its royal-blue glow was illuminating the bedroom. I glanced at my mother, her hand was still outstretched.

"Quickly, into the portal." She said.

"No, mum, you're coming with me."

"Of course, after you," she glanced over her shoulder at my father.

"Go!" my father yelled just as an orange spell hit him, silencing him.

My mother pushed me toward the portal.

"No—wait—Dad—"

"No time," my mother said frantically. "Kieran, we love you."

My eyes widened and my brows pulled together. Before I could utter a single word, she shoved me into the portal.

⋙ ◉ ⋘

DARKNESS. All I could see was the black forest I now stood in. I whipped around, observing my surroundings.

I was alone with no reminiscence of my mother's portal. The realisation that my mother hadn't made it through the portal hit me. My heart pounded heavily in my chest, my breathing uneven.

My father had sacrificed himself in an attempt my mother and I would get away. He had never been supportive of me learning how to be a Soul Weaver, but his sacrifice in the end somehow made up for it. But, my mother wasn't here. *Did she not make it to the portal? Had she taken a different portal? Had she never intended on coming with me?* I should have grabbed her hand and pulled her through with me. I should have learnt how to protect her.

I collapsed against a tree trunk, staring ahead at the dark trees in front of me. With no idea where I was or what to do now, I leaned my head back on the bark. I was thankful it was a warm night; otherwise, the shirt and shorts I wore wouldn't be ideal and my bare feet would be frozen. Without any breeze, an owl hooting nearby, and no moon shafts through the canopy, it was very eerie.

After what seemed like hours of sitting on the dirty forest floor, I willed myself to move. I walked through the trees with no idea where I was going. Glancing up into the canopy, I searched for any sign of direction; but there was nothing except thick leaves.

A branch snapped nearby. I whipped my head around wildly, searching the dark trees. I moved my feet faster; anxiety growing. With still no clue where I was or where to go, I hoped I was traveling in the right direction. *Was there ever going to be an end to this forest?*

Kicking my toe, I leant forward to grasp it, but I hit my forehead. I stared ahead, frozen in place. Lifting my hand, palm flat and facing away from my body, I slowly stretched out to touch the air. My hand flattened in midair — on an invisible wall.

Eyes widening, my heart pounding behind my ribs, I touched the invisible wall with both hands. It felt like glass, yet I couldn't see anything there. I ran my hands up and down it; it went all the way to the ground and higher than I could reach. I spun around toward the direction I had come and reached out. My hands hit another wall. I didn't understand. *How did I walk through one wall but not through the other?*

Turning my head, I looked to either side of me. I stretched my arms out from the sides of my body, but I didn't fully stretch out before I hit two more invisible walls. Dread washed over me. I was trapped in an invisible square cage. I punched my fist on the wall in front of me — I was instantly thrown backward and slammed into the opposite wall. I groaned as I stretched my back out.

A bush nearby rustled, and another branch broke. I stared in the sound's direction, squinting through the darkness.

"Who's there?" I called.

A youthful woman dropped from a nearby tree; she landed lightly on her feet as if she had floated down. My mouth hung open as I stared at her.

"Clara is my name." She ran her fingers through her short purple and black hair as she stepped forward.

I eyed her up and down. Long black boots covered her feet, black tights hugged her legs, and a long loose dark-green top covered her torso with a studded belt around on her hips.

"I'm—."

"I know who you are." She interrupted me.

I stared into her grey eyes, "how do you know me?"

"I was at your house, took longer than expected to find you."

I stumbled backward and hit the invisible wall behind me.

"You were with that man who attacked us?"

Her brow furrowed, "no, but sounds like you can describe him."

I glanced at a tree behind her, lost in thought about the appearance of that man. He had been no older than my parents.

"My parents... are they okay?" I asked.

She held up a hand toward me, yellow energy erupted from her hand. I swallowed, staring at the magic sweeping from her palm. It swirled and licked at the invisible wall for a moment, and then it evaporated.

"Come, you have much to discuss." She stated.

My eyebrows twitched as I looked around.

"You can move now," she said, shrugging. "Can never

be too cautious."

I nodded, understanding. Stepping forward, the air in front of me was clear again.

"Where are we going?"

"Myrdreya."

My mother spoke of the glass city often—maybe she had been right all along. Suspended high in the sky, the floating glass island had been created hundreds of years ago. They designed it to train us how to use and control our magic, and to provide us safety in a cruel world.

Clara's hand erupted with yellow energy again as she reached toward a nearby tree. The magic swirled and grew into an oval-shaped portal. I stared at the mesmerising gateway to the city; I could barely discern a glass bridge in the yellow.

"After you." Clara said, gesturing her hand toward it.

Swallowing, I stepped forward. I took a breath and stepped through. As I stepped out of the portal, the sun rays peeped between the clouds, shining upon the glass city before me. Myrdreya—finally.

"Welcome, home." Clara said.

About the Author

Chantelle Lambert grew up on the Sunshine Coast, Queensland, Australia. She spent much of her childhood on the Sunshine Coast before moving to Brisbane for her high school years. When she was nineteen, she moved states to the Central Coast of New South Wales where she met her husband, Ryan.

They have a beautiful daughter together who inspired her to chase her dream as a writer.

Chantelle spent a lot of her time growing up writing short stories and going off into the imaginative world. She loves the magical fantasy world in particular. She has read so many fantasy books, which have been her inspiration over the years to keep writing and to follow her dreams.

Her passion for writing and history of anxiety and depression lead her to write this fantasy novel.

Connect with Chantelle online:

www.facebook.com/pg/chantellelambertauthor
www.chantellelambert.com.au

SOUL WEAVER DUOLOGY BOOK TWO

The second book of the fantasy romance duology only gets tastier!

Trixie's life becomes more complicated when she discovers the extent of her power within. She finds herself on a mission to search for the only woman who can help her —a woman who does not want to be found.

When Kieran is taken by a ruthless enemy—an enemy Trixie never knew existed, Trixie and Kieran are forced to battle their own demons that being apart brings.

Will Trixie ever get her beloved Kieran back or will he become another tragedy in her life's timeline?

In the second book of this fantasy romance duology, Trixie suffers heartbreak and betrayal, as well as forming a powerful new friendship.

Life as a Mother is not your ordinary How to Guide.

Do you want to read real experiences from a real mother's perspective that you can actually relate to? Or are you a mother-to-be and you want to know what it's really like? We get the unrealistic perspective of motherhood everywhere, and we find ourselves going in blind. We see motherhood as being full of smiles and happiness, but it is so much more than that. It's also full of tears, fears, anger, boredom, and loneliness — not to mention depression and anxiety on top of everything else.

Being a mother is a miracle come true. It's very special — but it's also a nightmare. Your life will never be the same again — ever!

Together we will find our feet, we will hold each other's hand in the dark times of motherhood, and we will find the light.